'Now there's a laugh I haven't heard in a long time.' A deep, masculine voice spoke from behind her.

Eden froze, recognising it instantly. 'David.' His name was a whisper on her lips, and one she enjoyed hearing there. Goosebumps spread up and down her arms and she breathed in, trying not to sigh as the sweet and hypnotic scent she would always associate with David assailed her senses. The spicy scent had driven her wild at the age of seventeen, when they'd first got together. Actually, it was starting to drive her wild now. It was amazing that such a thing as scent could still affect her after a whole decade. He might have broken her heart, but that was then…this was now.

Slowly Eden turned, their gazes meeting. He stood in the doorway, all neat and tidy and as sexy as all get out. Eden let her gaze wander over his lithe frame, knowing he was doing exactly the same thing to her…she could feel it. Could he see the woman she'd grown into? Did he see much difference from the seventeen-year-old she'd been when he'd last seen her? She certainly hoped so.

Lucy Clark is a husband-and-wife writing team. They enjoy taking holidays with their two children, during which they discuss and develop new ideas for their books using the fantastic Australian scenery. They use their daily walks to talk over characterisation and fine details of the wonderful stories they produce, and are avid movie buffs. They live on the edge of a popular wine district in South Australia, and enjoy spending family time together at weekends.

Recent titles by the same author:

A MOTHER FOR HIS TWINS
CHILDREN'S DOCTOR, CHRISTMAS BRIDE
CITY SURGEON, OUTBACK BRIDE
A WEDDING AT LIMESTONE COAST
SURGEON BOSS, BACHELOR DAD

BRIDE ON THE CHILDREN'S WARD

BY
LUCY CLARK

⊚™ MILLS & BOON®

First published in Great Britain 2009
Large Print edition 2010
Harlequin Mills & Boon Limited,
Eton House, 18-24 Paradise Road,
Richmond, Surrey TW9 1SR

© Anne and Peter Clark 2009

ISBN: 978 0 263 21079 8

Printed and bound in Great Britain
by CPI Antony Rowe, Chippenham, Wiltshire

BRIDE ON THE CHILDREN'S WARD

To Natalie & Chris.
Congratulations.
Embrace your new life together.
Mark 5:19

CHAPTER ONE

EDEN couldn't believe the apprehensive nervousness clouding her as she entered the hospital and made her way to the spinal ward.

She was back.

Back home in one of Sydney's most exclusive suburbs, walking through the halls of the hospital she'd been born in twenty-nine years ago. She'd fled under the cover of darkness ten years earlier, and until two weeks ago hadn't made any plans ever to return. Australia was quite a way from where she'd been only a few days ago, but nevertheless she'd promised Sasha, her best friend, she would come home—and come home she had.

She glanced at a few people as she walked down the hospital's corridor, wondering if she would recognise anyone or if, heaven forbid, anyone could recognise her. Subconsciously, she knew she was hoping to see David walking towards her.

Did he know she was here? Had Sasha told him? Eden's heart-rate increased at the thought of David Montgomery—Sasha's older brother. He was the man she measured every other man against, and no one had yet lived up to the standards of tall, dark and handsome David.

When Eden had left home, only sweet Sasha had known her plans. The two had remained in constant contact over the years, their friendship never waning. They'd shared their deepest secrets from the moment they'd met when they were ten years old. Eden's leaving hadn't changed that. They'd written letters, and Sasha had visited her quite a few times. First in Darwin, where Eden had done her medical degree, and later overseas, where Eden had been working for Pacific Medical Aid, a medical relief organisation.

Swallowing over her dry throat, she felt another prickle of apprehension wash over her…as though someone was watching her. She looked behind her, but the corridor was empty. No David anywhere. Disappointed, she shook her head and chided herself for looking for him. David was a busy doctor and was no doubt somewhere in the hospital busy doing doctor

duties. He didn't have time to stand around cor-
ridors looking for her…did he?

Laughing nervously, she clutched the present
for Sasha tightly to her chest and turned left into
another long corridor. There was an information
board on the wall and she stopped momentarily
to make sure she was going the right way. Yes.
The spinal unit should be the second corridor on
the right.

The butterflies returned, but she reminded
herself it was just Sasha. She was here for Sasha.
Not David—the man who had broken her heart
all those years ago. Sure, she'd been young, and
he'd been her first serious boyfriend, but just as
a girl never forgot her first real kiss, she'd never
forgotten her first heartbreak either.

Sasha. She had to focus on Sasha. Not David,
not her parents or brother or anyone else in the
exclusive suburb where she'd done most of her
growing up. She was here for Sasha because that
was what best friends were for.

When she was finally standing outside Sasha's
door, Eden paused and brushed her free hand
down her skirt. It had been two and a half years
since she'd last seen Sasha. Eden had been
working in Ethiopia when Sasha and Robert,

Sasha's then fiancé, had come for a visit. It had been the first time Eden had met the man who had stolen her friend's heart, and she'd been delighted with him. The three of them had made lots of good memories during that visit, and for Eden it had been absolutely wonderful to see her friend so happy.

Then, a few months after their visit, Eden's world had exploded once again. Pain and anguish washed over her as pictures of that time flashed before her eyes, but she quickly pushed the awful memories from her mind, focusing instead on being able to do something for her friend. She had come because Sasha needed her.

Thank God Sasha had survived the horrific car accident which had now left her a patient in the spinal ward. Life wasn't fair—they both knew that—but at least Eden still had her best friend.

Hitching her handbag onto her shoulder, Eden knocked on the door before pushing it open and looking into the private room. She frowned. It was empty. She walked back towards the nurses' station and looked over the patient information board to make sure she had the right room. Yes. Room 4 was where Sasha Litchfield should be. Eden went back into the room and sighed.

All that anxiety and trepidation wasted. She laughed brightly at her own ridiculousness and put the bag and present down before heading over to the window, gazing out at the view of a small courtyard garden below.

'Now, there's a laugh I haven't heard in a long time.' A deep, masculine voice spoke from behind her.

Eden froze, recognising it instantly. 'David.' His name was scarcely a whisper on her lips, and one she enjoyed hearing there. Goose bumps spread up and down her arms and she breathed in, trying not to sigh as the sweet and hypnotic scent she would always associate with David assailed her senses. That spicy scent had driven her wild at the age of seventeen, when they'd first got together. Actually, it was starting to drive her wild now. It was amazing that such a thing as the mere smell of him could still affect her after a whole decade. He might have broken her heart, but that was a long time ago. That was then…this was now.

Slowly Eden turned. Their gazes met. He stood in the doorway, all neat and tidy, and as sexy as all get out. Eden let her gaze wander over his lithe frame, knowing he was doing exactly the

same thing to her...she could feel it. Could he
see the woman she'd grown into? Did he see
much difference from the seventeen-year-old
she'd been when he'd last seen her? She certainly hoped so.

'Well...' David was the first of them to find
his voice. 'Eden Caplan.' There was a veiled
twinkle in his brown eyes and the slight hint of
a smile on his lips. 'I thought I saw you in the
corridor just now.'

Eden spread her arms wide, her heart starting
to beat a different rhythm. 'It's me. In the flesh.'

'So I see.' His gaze dipped briefly to her knit
top which had a V-neckline. Eden smiled as his
Adam's apple worked up and down and he swallowed.

She quirked an eyebrow. 'Should I turn around?
Give you the full view?' She couldn't quite
believe she was flirting with him the way she had
in the past. Instantly, she felt as though she was
seventeen all over again, teasing him, wanting to
make him laugh. He'd always been so serious.

David was startled just for an instant, but
quickly recovered. He should have known to
expect something like that from Eden...the girl
who had provided such a bright spark to his oth-

erwise staid life all those years ago. 'Still saying the most outrageous things, I see.'

'Still stating the obvious, I see.'

He took a step farther into the room. 'It must be what…twelve years?'

Eden nodded. 'Your nineteenth birthday. Remember?'

He swallowed again and put his hands in his trouser pockets. 'I remember.' There was an air of determined nonchalance about him, as though he didn't want her to see how her words were affecting him. Was it possible that she could still knock the ever-steady David Montgomery off balance? She hoped so.

'You broke my heart.' She said the words with a hint of jest.

'I remember.'

'You broke my seventeen-year-old little heart and then you fled to Melbourne. Two years later, I fled—due to my own circumstances—and went to Darwin.'

'Opposite ends of Australia.'

'Until now.'

'Until now,' he repeated, and nodded his head slowly. There was a pause, which neither of them rushed to fill. It was as though they were both

swept back to the last time they'd been together—
that night in the depths of the Montgomerys'
enormous garden—where, beneath the moonlight, Eden had kissed David for the last time.
Kissed him goodbye with all the passion and
wonder of a seventeen-year-old in the throes of
her first love. Back then she'd thought they'd be
together for ever. That they'd be able to overcome
the objections of both his and her parents and
live happily ever after. Wasn't that what all
seventeen-year-old girls thought?

As though catching himself, David shook his
head and gestured to the empty bed. 'Sasha
finally got you here.'

Eden instantly became serious and concerned,
knowing he wouldn't sugar coat the truth. He
was David—the most honest man she'd ever
known. 'How is she, David?'

'Coping. It's been two weeks since the
accident, and medically she'll be fine. There's
still quite a bit of bruising, but that is fading. Of
course they say she'll never walk again, but you
and I know Sasha's determination. She'll prove
them wrong.' His tone was that of an experienced doctor, but Eden knew him far too well to
miss the slight tremor in his voice.

'You'd better believe it. Sasha's a fighter. I'm just sorry I couldn't get here earlier. For the past two weeks I've been getting daily updates from Robert. They've been like a lifeline to me.'

'Well, you're here now. I guess that's what counts.'

Eden sighed and shook her head, looking at the empty bed. 'Poor Sasha.'

'Uh, sorry. That's not allowed.' David took his hands out of his pockets and ticked the points off on his fingers. 'No pity, no lies, no looking back. Those are her rules.'

Eden grinned through the tears which had gathered behind her eyes. 'That sounds like my Sasha. Determined to find the silver lining and remain positive.'

'*And* we're allowed to spoil her as much as we want.'

'Oh, thank goodness. For a moment there I thought she'd gone totally off her rocker.'

David smiled, and she found it difficult not to sigh. He had the most gorgeous smile. It had always made her heart flutter and now was no exception. 'I'm glad you're here for her, Eden. It'll mean a lot to her.'

'Hey, that's what best friends are for. I'd do anything for Sasha.'

'Yet you didn't make it to her wedding two years ago.'

Eden's smile faltered at his words and she looked away, flicking her long auburn curls over her shoulder. Why had he brought that up? 'Sasha understood.'

David could see walls going up around her. Eden? Walls? She'd used to be an open book—especially to him. Then again, it had been twelve years, and people could certainly change a lot in twelve years. Himself included. 'Yes, she did. I didn't.'

Eden shrugged, not about to discuss one of the blackest period of her life. Not here, not now, and not with David. He'd always seen her as a strong person, and at that point she'd been anything but strong. Now, though, she was here for Sasha—to help her friend be strong, to listen and to make her laugh. That was her role because that was what best friends did.

Eden glanced towards the bed and picked up the nursing chart, scanning it briefly.

'You're not allowed to read that.' He sounded as though he didn't really care, but as David always did the right thing he probably felt he had to say the words out loud, even though he knew he wouldn't be able to stop her.

'So sue me,' she muttered.

'Got good malpractice insurance?'

'Doesn't everyone?' She glanced up at him and smiled, the uncomfortable moment over. 'Why? You want to borrow some of mine?'

'You'll share?'

'If I'm allowed to—which I don't think I am. But, hey, it's yours if you want it.'

David chuckled. 'Still the same old Eden. Confusing, baffling, but always amusing.'

Her smile brightened as the sound of his laughter washed over her. She tried not to sigh with repressed longing. She'd always loved his laugh, and here she was, years later, still enjoying the way it made her feel...the way *he* made her feel.

'Thank you, Dr Montgomery. I aim to please.' She returned the chart to its rightful place and prowled around the room, straightening the bedsheets so they'd be ready when Sasha returned. She could feel his gaze on her, watching her movements.

'I have to say that when Sasha told me you were studying medicine I was surprised.'

'Didn't think I was smart enough?'

'It was never a question of intelligence, Eden. No, I always thought you'd end up as a lawyer. Righting wrongs. Saving the oppressed. Doing your duty.'

'And you don't think medicine covers any of that?'

He thought for a moment. 'I guess it does, but in a different way.' Silence reigned again before he asked, 'So, what made you decide on medicine?'

'Your influence.' Eden's words were honest. 'Watching your dedication during your first year of med school, helping you swot for your exams. I was intrigued.'

It was because she'd helped him study for his first-year exams that they'd become closer friends. He'd started to see her as a person in her own right, rather than just a friend of his sister's. And then one night, when they'd been exhausted from studying and punch-drunk from too much caffeine, they'd kissed. His mouth on hers. It had been the most seductive and alluring kiss of his entire life…and he hadn't wanted it to end.

He'd known his parents didn't approve of Eden, of her influence over himself and Sasha, but he hadn't cared. She had been so vibrant, so radiant, that he'd been drawn to her like a moth to a flame. She'd brought sunshine into his life and he'd wanted it to remain. So they'd secretly started to date.

'I remember being surprised that you wanted to help. You had your own studying, your own homework to get through, your own high school exams.'

Eden waved his words away. 'They were easy. The medical world was exciting and different and I liked being able to help you out.' It had also given them the excuse they'd needed to spend time together.

Eden had always liked to be of help whenever she could, and when she'd realised that David didn't have a study partner she had offered her services and hadn't taken no for an answer. At first he'd thought it was simply so she could be near him, and whilst that was definitely a benefit, he'd been impressed when she'd proved herself to be a more than capable study partner.

David continued to watch her as she once more prowled around the room, glancing out of the window, straightening the different vases of flowers, making sure the sheets had perfect 'hospital corners'. Was she nervous? Had coming home after all this time made her nervous? Was *he* making her nervous? Did he still have the power to affect her? He wasn't sure how that made him feel. It was definitely something he could ponder later on.

'I take it Sasha's either in radiology or hydrotherapy, or having some other tests and she's going to come back wiped out and exhausted?'

David nodded. 'More than likely.'

'Seriously, David. How *is* she? From the big brother perspective, not the medical one, please.'

David's tone softened, and she could hear the love he had for his little sister in his words. 'She's coping, which is to be expected because that's the type of person she is, but the scars run deep, Eden. I'm expecting her to coast along for a few months and then come crashing down in a heap.'

Eden nodded. She'd seen it before—far too many times to count. 'It's to be expected. Her life's been spun in a circle, chopped in half and then flipped upside down.'

'You sound as though you know something of that.'

'Well, I could hardly be expected to stay the

same person I was when I left. A lot can happen to a girl from nineteen to twenty-nine.'

'She becomes a woman.' His words were soft, caressing, and Eden had to stop herself from crossing the room and planting a big, smoochy kiss on those delicious lips of his. David had been the only man who had ever affected her like this. The sound of his voice, the scent of his cologne, the way he held himself. Everything about the man made her want to be reckless and exuberant, yet at the same time she couldn't forget that he'd broken her heart once before—which meant he was more than capable of doing it again.

There was another one of those pauses, but this time neither of them rushed to fill the gap. It was as though simply being in the same room was enough for now. There was a lot that hadn't been said between them, and she hoped during this visit she'd finally be able to get some perspective on things where David was concerned. He was definitely an unfinished chapter in her life, and she was very interested in finding out how it would end.

He cleared his throat. 'I've…er…read your papers. They're very good.'

That surprised her. 'Really?' Did he have any idea how much it meant to hear him say something like that?

David chuckled. 'That's what happens when you publish them in medical journals, Eden.'

'I guess. But that wasn't the reason I wrote them.'

'Not for the prestige? Not interested in making a big name for yourself?'

'No. That may surprise you, but it's the truth.'

'So you're content to hide away in some Third World country, caring for the sick and then writing about it?'

'As well as trying to educate other doctors,' she felt compelled to point out. 'And I'm hardly hiding, David.'

'Where are you based now?'

'The Ukraine. A small village about two hours outside Kiev.'

'And how long are you back for?'

'I'm not sure. It all depends on Sasha.' She had been devastated that she hadn't been able to get back to Australia for Sasha's wedding, and this time, when her friend needed her, she had been determined to be there. To help—because that was what Eden did. She helped people. If she kept herself busy, if she focused on helping others to get better, then it meant she didn't need to focus on herself.

'Good to hear. You've come back just in time for a fairly decent Sydney spring.'

Eden shrugged. 'Actually, the temperature isn't that much different from the Ukrainian autumn.'

He nodded, still unable to believe she was really here. He'd thought about her a lot over the years—more than she would ever know—but he'd also accepted that Eden Caplan was nothing more than a long-ago romance. He was, however, surprised to find that being near her, standing close to her and inhaling her wild perfume, still elicited a reaction from his body.

His pager beeped and he quickly glanced at the number. 'Well…I guess we'll be seeing each other quite a bit whilst you're here.'

'I guess we will.' As she spoke, her eyes dipped down to rest on his mouth. The memory of those lips pressed against hers flashed into her mind. The kisses they'd shared had happened so long ago, yet standing near him now it felt as though it was only last week. How could twelve years disappear so quickly, yet the feelings and emotions remain? What would it be like, she wondered, to feel that mouth on hers once more?

He cleared his throat. 'I'd...better get to the ward.'

At his words, Eden immediately looked away, feeling slightly embarrassed.

'Do you want me to find out how much longer Sasha will be?' he offered.

'No, that's fine.' She waved his words away. 'You go. I can speak to the nurses, introduce myself, get a cup of coffee. That sort of thing.'

David nodded. 'OK.' He still didn't move. 'I guess I'll see you later.'

Eden's smile was bright. 'I guess you will.'

David didn't move. He was mesmerised by the way her green eyes twinkled with happiness, and for a second he wanted to believe that it was happiness at seeing him again. Her mouth was curved in that delicious way which had always urged him to kiss it—and he realised that now was no exception.

He closed his eyes for a moment and slowly shook his head. 'Don't do that, Eden.'

'Do what?' The smile faded. What had she done?

'Don't smile at me like that.' He didn't want her to affect him the way she did. He didn't want to stare at her mouth the way she'd been staring at his. He wanted to be immune to her smiles, to her expressive eyes, to the way her body seemed to sway and radiate a love of life. Here she was, the girl who had definitely grown into a woman…and she was *still* affecting him. He'd left town all those years ago to escape his constant thoughts about her, to put temptation right out of the way. And now, over twelve years later, she was back—and the connection between them was not only still there but apparently as strong as ever.

'My smile? You're cross when I smile?'

He raked a hand through his hair. 'Yes.'

'Why? It's just a smile, David.'

'No, Eden. It's *your* smile. That *come hither* smile.' His voice was low and a little shaky, showing Eden just how much she could affect him. It surprised her.

'Do you want me to…come hither?' Her tone was equally intimate.

'No.' He took a step backwards as though to prove his point. 'We're grown-ups now. We can control our emotions much better than when we were teenagers.'

She wasn't too sure about that. A few minutes in his company had revealed that she was still as strongly attracted to him now as she'd been as a teenager, and apparently she wasn't alone in her feelings.

Again they both stood there, almost as though they were sizing each other up, drawing the boundary lines... Well, David certainly was. He needed to guard his heart, to guard his words and to guard his unwanted attraction to Eden. He'd made a fool of himself in the past and he'd vowed he'd never let it happen again. One failed marriage was enough for a man to live with— and besides, the reason for his marriage break-up was still very relevant.

He'd do well to keep her at arm's length during her stay and not get involved, despite the signals his body was sending to his brain. Flirting and getting involved with Eden Caplan was the last thing he needed—especially now, when he was determined to prove himself as the new head of Paediatrics.

His pager beeped again, bringing him back to reality.

'You're obviously very popular,' she murmured.

David knew he should go, knew he *had* to go, but again he found it hard to leave her presence. He opened his mouth to say something, decided better of it, closed his lips together, gave her a brisk nod and turned on his heel, striding from his sister's hospital room. To say anything else to Eden would just continue to wind him in knots.

He hadn't been prepared to see her, even though Sasha had told him she'd been in contact with Eden. Still he hadn't expected her to come. She hadn't bothered to come for Sasha's wedding, which David had found extremely odd. Or perhaps it was just that he had been mentally psyching himself up to see her, interested to see whether the frightening natural chemistry which had existed between them in the past was still there. And then he'd been let down by her lack of appearance.

As soon as Sasha had announced her engagement to Robert, David had thought Eden would come home. It had been the day before Sasha's wedding when his sister had told him that Eden would be unable to make it. Still, he'd half expected Eden to show up on the day, in a flurry of colour, but she hadn't—and he'd been angry with himself for caring. That had turned into anger aimed at Eden for not being there on her best friend's special day.

'Well, she's here now,' he muttered. 'And you

certainly weren't prepared.' He shook his head, feeling a lot like an adolescent schoolboy, unable to control his body's reaction to a beautiful girl. Which was exactly the predicament he'd found himself in all those years ago when they'd first kissed.

He'd known she'd had a crush on him, and whilst he'd been flattered, he'd known it was up to him to ensure they kept their distance. Dating his sister's best friend would only lead to disaster. Besides that, he'd had medical school ahead of him, and Eden Caplan would have ended up being an enormous distraction with a capital D.

Then, when she'd offered to study with him, he'd accepted—even though he'd known he was playing with fire. He'd managed to keep things on an even keel until after she'd been helping him study for over two months. Then one night, tired from studying so much, Sasha long since having fallen asleep on her brother's bed, David had given in to the irrepressible urge to feel his lips against Eden's.

She had waited patiently for him to make that first move, but once he had she hadn't held back. He'd been astounded at the surge of emotions he'd felt upon kissing her. Even then he'd still fought against the attraction, knowing his parents wouldn't approve of Eden, but he'd been helpless. Eventually he'd agreed to date her, so long as it was kept from their parents.

He shook his head, wondering how they could have been so stupid. 'Nineteen and thinking you knew it all,' he scolded himself with a half laugh, shaking his head at their teenage naïveté. Still, the time they'd spent together had been so freeing for him—especially given that his home life hadn't been all that happy. Then, at his nineteenth birthday party, David's father had informed him that the rest of his medical schooling would be completed in Melbourne, rather than Sydney. When he'd asked why, his father had bluntly stated that it was to get David away from trash like Eden Caplan.

David had tried to argue, to state that the grades for his recent exams wouldn't have been so high if it hadn't been for Eden, but his father had simply dismissed him. So David had found Eden, taken her out to the garden so they could be alone, and then broken her heart.

He hadn't been able to tell her the truth about his parents' decision because he'd been so embarrassed and ashamed by their snobbery. He'd known if he'd confessed the real reason why he was leaving, Eden would stand up and fight against it. That she would no doubt lobby his parents to get them to change their minds, to show them how unfair they were being. But he'd known his parents' controlling indifference far too well, and known that if he allowed Eden to do that it would mean the end of her friendship with Sasha…and Sasha had needed Eden more than he had.

So he'd told her it was over between them. Told her he was leaving because he needed to devote more time to studying. That she was a distraction, that his life didn't have room for her in it. She hadn't cried, even though he'd seen quite clearly that she wanted to. Instead, she'd kissed him, so passionately, so intimately that it was as though he could still feel the touch of her lips on his now. Then she'd fled.

Now, though, Eden was back—and so were the memories. Her scent was the same. Her laugh was the same. Her rich, green eyes were as hypnotic now as then. His heart-rate accelerated. He couldn't believe his reaction to her was the same as it had been well over a decade ago.

Well, of one thing he was certain. He couldn't

change the past, but he could certainly learn from it—and that meant better control over his future.

Eden was only in town for a few weeks, and he would have to keep all contact with her down to the absolute minimum. They were older now, and their careers would keep them headed in different directions. He'd lived through some intense events. He'd worked his way methodically through them and was still dealing with others. He wasn't the same man he'd been at the age of nineteen… Yet seeing Eden standing framed against the sunlight coming from the window had stirred something deep within him which he'd thought long since dormant.

She wouldn't be here long. She had her own life. He had his. He *could* resist her…and he would. With his mind firmly back on track, David took the stairs two at a time as he headed to the paediatric ward to check on his little patients.

As he walked in, a flash of blue ran in his direction before wrapping around his legs. David looked down in surprise. 'Dart?'

'They want to give me yucky meddy. I don't like yucky meddy, Dr David.'

David looked up to find Francie, one of the

nursing sisters on the ward, standing there with her palms spread wide. 'He's too quick for me,' she said with a grin as she headed towards them.

David managed to pry Dart's hands from his legs and bent down so he was closer to the four-year-old's height. 'I don't like yucky medicine either, Dart.'

Dart's blue eyes widened. 'You don't?'

'No, but sometimes swallowing the yucky medicine is the only way our bodies can get better.' David stood and held out his hand to the boy. 'Let's get you back to your bed and I'll check your chart.'

Dart trustingly took David's hand and went happily back to his bed, where he bounced around on his hands and knees. Francie was there beside him, trying to get Dart to quieten down. 'Have you been bouncing around like this all morning long?' David asked Dart.

'I'm feeling so good today that I don't even *need* to have the yucky meddy.'

'Is that right?' David nodded wisely, but couldn't help the niggling feeling that he was missing something. 'Temperature normal all night long. And you've managed to eat all your breakfast.'

'I was hungry,' Dart interjected.

'These are all good signs.'

A grin split the little boy's face. 'And *that's* why I don't need to have any yucky meddy.'

David couldn't help but laugh. 'You're a persistent one.'

'I am.' Dart stopped bouncing for a second and tilted his head to the side. 'What's *sersistent* mean?'

'Persistent. It means you don't give up.' Dart merely shrugged his shoulders and started bouncing around again. 'In fact,' David continued, 'if you keep on getting better we might be able to let you go home tomorrow. Where's your mum? I'll go and have a chat with her now.'

David winked at the little boy and went in search of his mother. Mrs Wilman was always around. She was one of those parents who insisted on spending all of her time in hospital with her son, wanting to care for him as much as possible. It was strange that she wasn't around now.

'Ah…Mrs Wilman had to go home last night. Her husband called to say he was in town for a brief visit and wanted to take his wife out to dinner. I told her to go—in fact, I had to almost pressure her to go. Dart was doing fine. The woman needs a break every now and then. Anyway, she should be back within the hour. Apparently, her husband had to fly off to Prague this morning.'

'He travels a lot?'

'Yes. From what I understand, from what she's told me, he's an international businessman. Not really sure exactly what he does, but he's away ninety percent of the time.'

'That can't make it easy on her. Raising a bubbly four-year-old on her own.' David read Dart's case notes, which were kept at the nurses' station. 'Did Dart's father come to see him last night?'

'No. Mrs Wilman said that as it was only a flying visit she didn't want Dart upset at not being able to spend more time with his father.'

David nodded, frowning a little as he read about Dart's previous two admissions. One had been when he'd just turned three—almost eighteen months ago. The boy had fallen out of a tree and broken his arm. The fracture had been a greenstick, but he'd been kept in for over a week. The second admission had been just four months ago.

Back then David had taken a shine to the little boy who had presented with a multitude of symptoms. Dehydration, iron deficiency and slight malnutrition. This time Dart's symptoms had been somewhat similar, the malnutrition more severe. Mrs Wilman was concerned that Dart was hiding his food, that he was somehow not eating what she provided. She would give him drinks, but for all she knew he was tipping them into the garden.

After a week in hospital, the first twenty-four hours having seen the little boy on a drip to boost his fluids and get his system back on track, Dart had made a brilliant improvement.

'What do you want me to do with the yucky meddy?' Francie asked, a small smile on her lips.

'Watch him. See how he is. Do his obs for the next few hours, and if he starts to go down, call me. If he can do without the medicine and his body is functioning fine, then we'll leave it at that.' David wrote those instructions in Dart's notes before getting started on his informal ward round.

Once he was done, he headed to his office to return some phone calls. He was pleased that he'd managed to not think about Eden for almost a whole hour, and reminded himself that when he focused on work any diversion could be controlled.

As he rounded the corner, he slammed straight

into the one woman he didn't want to slam into. 'Eden.' His arms came around her to steady both of them. The scent of her wild perfume swirled around him, wiping all coherent thought from his mind. The last time he'd held her like this he'd ended up being unable to resist her charms. His first instinct was to put as much distance between them as possible, and he meant to do just that. Yet all he seemed capable of managing was to shift his hands from her waist to her arms.

'Sorry,' she mumbled, her head down, her hair shielding her face. She sniffed, and that was the first inclination he had that something was wrong.

'Eden? What is it? What's wrong?'

She looked up at him. He hadn't removed his hands from her arms, and all she wanted right at that moment was to lean close to him, to feel his arms about her, giving the comfort she was so desperate to receive.

'I'm sorry, David. It's fine.'

'It's obviously not.' He propelled her into his office. Once inside, he shut the door and turned her to face him. Her nose was shiny and red, her eyes were glazed and her cheeks were ruddy. 'You've been crying!'

Eden gave a pitiful laugh. 'Was it the tears

which gave it away, or my impersonation of Rudolph the Red-Nosed Reindeer?'

David put his hands on her shoulders. 'Rudolph, actually.' The attempt at humour was totally Eden, always trying to lighten a serious moment, and he gazed down into her eyes, his tone filled with compassion. 'What is it?'

'It's nothing. Honestly. I just thought I was sufficiently prepared, that's all. I wasn't, and now I'm paying for it.'

'Prepared? For what?'

'For *Sasha*!' Even as Eden said the words her eyes filled once more and her lower lip quivered. 'I've seen a lot of terrible and tragic sights in the past, but this…this is different. This is Sasha. *My* Sasha. I had no idea it was going to hit me like this.' She waved her arms about in the air. 'I mean—to see her like that. And in a wheelchair! I knew it was going to be like that, but it's real, David. It's *real*. My beautiful Sasha, my best friend…she's broken and I can't fix her.' The distress in Eden's voice was paramount and a fresh bout of tears followed.

Without a word, David pulled her into his arms and held her tight.

CHAPTER TWO

HE LET HER CRY. He simply held her and let her cry.

Eden felt safe and secure in his arms as he offered comfort. He knew what she was feeling, what she was experiencing be-cause he'd been there as well. David understood because Sasha was his sister. At the same time, Eden was acutely aware of how nice it was to be this close to him, to feel his warmth, to breathe in his scent. However, that wasn't the point of this embrace, and she tried to school her mind in the right direction.

She knew she needed to get herself together before seeing Sasha again. She needed to be strong, to be in control so her friend could lean on her.

'But you *are* strong.' David's words were filled with caring, and it was then that Eden realised she'd spoken out loud. 'You're the strongest woman I know.' He dragged in a breath, closing his eyes with pleasure as her scent continued to surround him. His fingers played with the ends of her hair, loving the silkiness of her curls. 'You're also the most stubborn and pigheaded,' he added softly, the tenderness in his tone belying the severity his words might have carried.

Eden sniffed, her tears starting to subside, but she made no attempt to draw back from David's arms. 'Some people consider those qualities an asset.'

'I never said they weren't.' He knew he was playing with fire, and that he'd no doubt get burnt, but he couldn't deny how nice it was to comfort her like this. Especially as he knew exactly how she felt—the helplessness at being unable to 'fix' Sasha.

Eden smiled at his words, shifting to press her ear to his chest, enjoying the lub-dub of his heartbeat. Her hands were still curled beneath her chin, but as she hiccuped a few times her breathing started to return to normal. Drawing in a deep breath, she let it out slowly and sighed.

David closed his eyes. He should let her go, step away, *move* before he did something they'd both regret... Well, something *he'd* regret. Eden had always been the sort of person to act on impulse, to speak her mind whenever she had something to say, and she had never apologised for being that way. Her directness was a quality he'd long admired, though he'd never told her that.

He needed to let her go. To put distance between them. But this was Eden…the only woman who'd ever managed to make him lose control over his usually logical thought processes. The only woman who fitted so perfectly into his arms. So perfect.

'Well, if you're feeling better I should let you go.' His voice was soft, quiet and very intimate.

She could hear something different in his tone. A hint of veiled desire, perhaps? Was the fact that she was standing this close to him, listening to his heartbeat, too much for him to fight? 'You should,' she whispered back. 'Although it sounds as though you don't want to.'

'Eden. We can't.'

'Can't what?'

'I think you know what.'

'Well, maybe I need you to spell it out for me?'

David dragged in one last deep breath, appreciating the feel of her so close, so near to him, before opening his eyes and finally releasing her. Eden dropped her hands to her sides, feeling instantly cold and bereft. She rubbed her hands up and down her arms.

'What can't we do, David?'

He was silent, looking down at her, his gaze drawn to her mouth…her full, highly kissable mouth.

'Pick up where we left off.' His eyes were intent on hers as he spoke, showing her that he wasn't shying away from the memories, but merely putting them into order.

His words surprised her. 'The last time I saw you was the night I kissed you goodbye.'

'I remember. You're…you, and you're… gorgeous, and…' He stopped and cleared his throat, trying to get a better handle on the situation. 'I don't think we need to go down that road again. We know where it leads.'

David forced himself to move, taking two giant steps backwards, and bumped directly into his desk. He placed a hand on the wood, feeling the hard reality of the world around them. 'Besides, I know you didn't come back home for me.'

Eden angled her head to the side, her red curls falling over her shoulder in a way that made him want to touch them. To feel the silky softness sift through his fingers. To breathe in her scent. To let himself go.

How did she do it? How could she make him forget everything? Everything except the frightening natural chemistry which existed between them. It was incredible that after twelve long years, their lives having taken them in completely different directions, the attraction was still there…still as powerful and as strong as ever.

'No. I didn't come home *just* to kiss you, David.'

'We've both changed a lot in the past twelve years. We're adults now, not teenagers, and I think we can control ourselves much better.'

'True.' Eden shifted and pondered his words for a moment. 'Although I thought the reason you ran away before was because I was so young, so inexperienced. Wasn't that the reason you gave me? You didn't want to hold me back from experiencing life, from dating other people, from having experiences I wouldn't have if I continued to date you? I was only seventeen. I was too young to be tied down, to be in a relationship.'

'You *were* so young, and that *was* the problem,' he stated firmly. 'Now, can we please drop the subject.'

He hadn't said anything confirming her being inexperienced. That was good. It was a concern Eden had been carrying around for such a long time. She'd often wondered what she had done wrong. She'd been so confused by his reaction. First he had pushed her away, and then he had returned the last kiss they'd shared. Then he'd not only put her from him but he'd left the *state*!

Back then, when she'd been in her late teens, Eden had hidden her true self behind humour, flippancy and her crusades in helping others. David's leaving had hurt her so much that the only way she'd been able to cope was to repress her pain, to close off that part of her. She'd cried herself to sleep for weeks on end, trying to figure out what she'd done wrong. Why had he left her? Why hadn't he wanted her?

Of course she'd hidden her feelings from everyone, locking them away. She'd been bright and bubbly on the outside, throwing herself into helping others. She'd volunteered at soup kitchens, helped out at a women's shelter, and when she'd graduated from high school the year after David had left, instead of being one of the party animals she'd been one of the carers, helping those who'd drunk too much to find a safe place to spend the night.

One crusade after another. Helping others wherever possible. It was the reason she'd become a doctor, wanting to be able to help those less fortunate than herself. Now here she was… almost full circle. Near David, breathing him in and still unsure what she should do. Did he have any idea what seeing him again had done to her? Awakening those feelings she'd thought long buried, deep down inside?

'And I didn't *run* away. My parents decreed that I should continue my studies in Melbourne, and as they held the money-strings, I went. Besides, it ended up being a good career move as the university there had a stronger focus on paediatrics. But I didn't *run* away.' He stood from where he was, leaning on his desk, and went around to sit in his chair, putting even more distance between them.

'So…just a second. Are you saying you broke up with me because your parents found out about us?'

'Yes.'

'You *didn't* want to end it, then?'

'Eden. It's in the past. Let it go.'

'Wait. Let me just clarify here. Are you saying

that you *did* like kissing me? That you liked hanging out with me, spending time with me? Dating me?'

'Yes.'

'You didn't break up with me because I wouldn't go all the way with you?'

'Eden! You know I was against us "going all the way". You were too young.'

'But you wanted to,' she pushed.

'Of course I did. We were dating and you're… *you*.' He shook his head and raked a shaking hand through his hair.

'You wanted me back then?'

'I did. Can we drop this now?'

'And you left because your parents made you?'

'Yes.'

'Then why didn't you tell me the truth? Why did you let me think you didn't care about me?'

'Because I cared about you *too* much. You and Sasha.' He shifted and looked her in the eyes. 'Look, Eden, I know you. I know you would have fought against my parents' decision, and then they would have banned you from seeing Sasha, done whatever else they could to destroy you as well. They're experts when it comes to getting what they want, and they wanted us apart. I figured telling you it was my idea would at least give you access to Sasha. She needed you more. She still does.'

Eden shook her head in wonder. 'All those years I thought I'd done something wrong, but now you tell me that wasn't the case.'

'You hadn't done anything wrong.'

'And *you* didn't think to fight your parents? To tell them you weren't going to go to Melbourne?'

'Not back then. I'm ashamed to admit it, but I was nineteen and to all intents and purposes I'd been sheltered for most of my life—even though my parents had so little to do with my upbringing.'

Eden smiled. 'You had a few nannies.'

'*I* didn't. Sasha did.'

'Right.' She smiled as though she didn't believe him, but it didn't matter any more. Although David *had* left her, had gone to Melbourne, it hadn't been *because* of her.

'Now, can we please leave it?'

She nodded. 'All right. Subject dropped.' She walked over to the chair opposite where he sat and lowered herself into it. 'So tell me…what's been happening with your life during the past twelve years?'

'I'm sure Sasha has kept you informed.'

Eden acknowledged his words with a slight nod. 'Not in great detail. She told me you were getting married—I cried myself to sleep that night.' She sighed theatrically so he didn't take her seriously. 'Then she mentioned you were getting divorced.'

'Did you cry that night, too?'

'I was sorry for you. Sorry that it hadn't worked out. You deserve happiness, David.' There were no theatrics now, just sincerity. 'Will you tell me what happened?'

'Nothing out of the ordinary. I married a woman I shouldn't have. Simple.'

'Who?'

'Jacqueline Baker. I don't think you know her. She wasn't from around here, but our parents knew each other through their charity work.'

'Ha! Charity work as far as our parents are concerned is throwing money at people, but never once getting their own hands dirty.' She blew on her nails. 'Oops. I've chipped my manicure.'

'As I was saying, Jacquie and I met through our parents. We became friends, and then we sort of drifted into marriage.'

'Drifted? Sounds terribly romantic.'

'Do you want me to tell you or not?'

'Yes. Sorry. I'll be quiet.'

'Thank you. After trying to make it work for about three years, we both decided we'd been stupid to allow ourselves to be pushed into the union and we amicably divorced. She's now re-married and is expecting her first child very soon.' He frowned as he said the words, and Eden knew there was certainly more to it than he was letting on.

'You still see her?'

'At social gatherings. She's been in a few times recently to see Sasha.'

'An amicable divorce. Isn't that an oxymoron?'

David smiled, but it didn't reach his eyes. 'It does happen. Jacquie and I were always better at the friends part, so that's the part we've kept, and although our divorce displeased our parents, we knew it was the right thing to do.'

'And you always do the right thing?'

'Not always, Eden.'

'Really?' She raised her eyebrows, a teasing glint in her eyes. 'Well, I look forward to the next time you decide to buck the system.'

'Stop it,' he said with a warning smile. 'I'm not

letting you bait me this time.' How was it that she had the ability to make him feel young and carefree again? It was so…Eden. So bright, so bubbly, but he'd been watching her before and had seen a multitude of emotions flit across her face, each one as brief as the next.

It reminded him of the nights she and Sasha had helped him study for exams. They would be all serious and studious one moment and then laughing the next. Those had been some of his favourite study sessions, and whilst Sasha had ended up falling asleep a lot of the time, leaving himself and Eden to slog through the workload, David had felt even then that there was a much deeper side to Eden than anyone realised.

'Party-pooper.' She gave a mock pout.

'Exactly. Now, speaking of parents, are you planning to see yours whilst you're back in town?' As he spoke, he watched as every muscle in her gorgeous body tensed. 'I take it your family are still a sore point.'

'Uh…yeah. I haven't spoken to any of them in ten years.'

'Is that so?' David knew this, as he was in fairly constant contact with her father, Hal, but now wasn't the time to tell Eden that.

'Come on, David. You know what my parents
are like. Money is the only thing important to
them. Oh, no—wait. Money and status. Two
things are important to them. Not the happiness
of their children.'

'Todd turned out all right.'

Eden almost pounced at the mention of her
little brother. There had been so many times—
especially in the first few years after she'd left
home—where she'd missed him terribly,
wishing he was with her. 'You've seen him? How
is he?'

'He's good, Eden, and I know he'd like to see
you.'

She eased back into her chair, watching him
carefully. 'You know this…how?'

'Because I see them quite regularly. Your
father is on the hospital board.'

'Of course he is.'

'And your mother is involved in several of the
same charities as my mother.'

'Accepted at last. She should be proud of herself.'

'They've changed, Eden. Don't you think it's
about time to put the past to rest?'

Eden brushed the hair back from her face,
letting David's words sink in. 'I wrote to Todd

not long after I left, and he wrote me a letter back saying he never wanted to speak to me again.'

'He was…what…fifteen years old then?'

'About that.'

'So what does a fifteen-year-old brother know? He was probably hurt.'

'I've sent my family Christmas and birthday cards every year, but never got one back.'

'Maybe they didn't know what to say?'

'How about "To Eden. Merry Christmas from your parents"?'

'Did they know where to send them?'

'They had the address of the agency.'

'Maybe things didn't get through to you?'

'The agency always passes on mail to staff. All of Sasha's letters and cards made it through. Besides, I was in Darwin at medical school for a lot of that time, and although I was working in the Outback during vacations they still could have contacted me.'

'Stop avoiding the question, Eden. Are you going to see them or not?'

'I don't know,' she huffed, and crossed her arms defensively over her chest. 'And stop being on their side. You were my friend first.'

'This isn't about sides, Eden.'

She closed her eyes and tried to calm herself down. Finally she looked at David and shrugged. 'I don't know what to do.'

'You must have known this question would arise when you decided to come back.'

'Yes, of course. But honestly, David, if I'd allowed myself to focus on that I might not have come. I'm here for Sasha. First and foremost.'

'No one's disputing that, but what's stopping you from healing this old wound? You've locked your family away in a box marked "DO NOT TOUCH". It's not healthy for them to stay there for the rest of your life.'

He had a point. What he didn't know was that she had a box with his name on it marked 'DO NOT TOUCH' as well, and yet here she was, sitting opposite him, drinking in the sight of him, allowing herself to be swayed by him. He'd always been able to make a convincing argument, and she had a feeling he wasn't going to let this one drop.

The worry, the concern and the repressed pain were clearly evident on her face. 'I don't know if I'm strong enough to handle more rejection from them.' She dropped her hands, dejection overcoming her with force. 'My father kicked me out, David. He told me to leave and to never come back.'

'He's changed, Eden.' David came around the desk, but still kept a clear distance between them. 'You're so driven, so focused, and you are always there for others. Be there for *them*.' His words were deep, imploring. 'Apart from all of that, I've already told you that you are the strongest woman I know.'

She sighed and gave him a small smile. 'And I thought that was because I used to beat you at arm wrestling.'

He matched her grin. 'I used to let you win.'

Her smile increased, her tension starting to dissipate. 'I know.'

David paused, his tone encouraging. 'See them, Eden. Perhaps now is the time to put the past behind you? To start afresh?'

'Next you'll be saying that life is too short to have regrets.'

'It is.'

'Do you have regrets?'

'Who doesn't?'

'I mean about me.' Eden's heart started pounding fiercely against her chest as she spoke. Could he see she wasn't joking around or teasing this time? Could he feel that she needed some sort of reassurance? He'd rejected her and it had hurt. Then he'd left, adding even more pain and guilt to the rejection she'd suffered.

David was silent, and she was about to tell him to forget it when finally he answered. 'Of course I do. But we were both so young.'

'You still rejected me, David. Rejection is never easy to handle. First you, then my family. Oh, I'd been used to being on the outside at school, in fact, ever since my parents moved to the "money" suburb after their lottery win, but rejection, especially at such a young and impressionable age, hurts.'

'I tried to let you down as gently as I knew how.'

'By leaving me? By cutting yourself off?'

'If I wasn't around, I knew it would protect both of us from heading in a direction which was—'

'Oh, you don't need to explain. I understand now, being older, but still, rejection is never easy to deal with. I would have gone completely around the bend if it hadn't been for Sasha. She was the only one, still *is* the only one, who's always been there for me. It's why I needed to come back. She needs me and I'm here.'

'Yet you didn't make it to her wedding.'

'We've discussed this, David.' There was a warning in her tone, a warning not to push her, but he needed to know.

'Not really, Eden. I still don't understand why you didn't come. It makes no sense. Too busy helping others? Researching? Writing papers? Couldn't that have waited? Your best friend got married and she wanted you there.'

'Sasha understood.'

'So you say.'

'No, David. Sasha *really* understood.'

'Then explain it to me.'

'I'd rather not, if you don't mind. I've been on enough of an emotional roller-coaster for one day and I don't need another turn.' She walked towards the door, eager to put some distance between them—for when he looked at her with such cold confusion Eden's heart started to break. She was far too vulnerable right now to discuss such a topic with him. Not only because it had been one of the darkest times in her life, but because she'd no doubt end up in tears again.

'I should get back and check on Sasha, or at

least chat to Robert if Sasha's sleeping. He's so perfect for her.' Eden's smile came naturally when she thought about the way Robert and Sasha looked at each other. Along with that smile came a natural yearning to one day experience that sort of love. Would she ever find the right man? Was he standing right in front of her?

She was changing the subject and David let her, but hopefully she'd realise he wasn't going to let the subject drop. It was important to him. He needed to understand, because not turning up for her best friend's wedding had been so unlike the Eden he thought he'd know. He didn't want to think he'd misjudged her character, that the young woman he'd distanced himself from was someone very different deep down inside. It was for that reason alone that he was determined to discover the real reason why she hadn't been there to share in Sasha's special day.

'Yes, he's good for Sasha. Loves her one hundred percent.'

'It's so rare to find that happily-ever-after, and I'm so glad it happened for Sasha. I know they've got a long and difficult road ahead of them, but I honestly believe they'll make it.'

David agreed. 'Rob's a patient man. He'll stand by her.'

Eden smiled. 'Must be good that he has your approval. Good for Sasha, I mean. Your opinion means so much to her.'

'Does it mean anything to you?'

'Your opinion?' Eden was a little surprised at the question. 'Of course. I value your opinion, David. I always have.' Didn't the man have *any* idea of the influence he'd had on her life? She had measured every other man she'd come across against David. He was her yardstick, and so far no one had ever come close to matching him in integrity, in honesty, in ethics or principles, and of course looks and sex appeal. David definitely had those last two in spades.

'Well…that's nice to know. Hopefully you'll trust me enough to tell me why you didn't make it back for the wedding.'

Eden's sigh was heavy and she gripped the door handle a little tighter. 'It's not that I don't trust you, David. It's just that…' She knew he wasn't going to let it go. He wanted an answer and he would eventually drag one from her. He was a man who, once he decided on something, usually followed through.

She rubbed at her temple with her free hand. 'It's just that it was a *very* difficult time in my life. But as I said, I've had enough emotion for now, and bringing it up would only make me upset again. I'd no doubt end up back in your arms and then we'd have to fight this…' she waved her hand about to indicate the space between them '…this chemistry thing which still exists between us. I don't have the energy for that. You say you've read my papers. Read them again, David, and this time read between the lines.'

It wasn't the answer he'd been expecting, and seeing the hint of raw pain and anguish in her eyes made him feel uneasy. He shouldn't have pushed so hard, so fast.

David nodded. 'I'll do that.'

'OK.' She opened the door, but stopped halfway through it. 'Oh, and I'm sorry about before. The crying thing.'

'No need to apologise. I understand.'

'Thanks.'

'Feeling stronger?'

Eden smiled, but it wasn't like the other smiles which had touched her eyes, and he knew he was the one who had taken that glow from her earlier spark. 'Back to my old self.'

'Heaven help us.' He rolled his eyes heaven-ward. 'Go see Sasha.'

He kept his encouraging smile in place until she'd gone, but the instant he was alone he closed his eyes and shook his head. Why did the woman affect him so much? She'd been here for less than an hour and already he was so tied up in knots he'd need a steamroller to squash them out. And then he'd gone and pushed her. He'd wanted to know, and all she'd left him with was a cryptic message and a sadness around her eyes.

He recalled numerous times when she had sent him out to collect petition signatures for one lost cause or another…and he'd done it. He also re-membered one occasion where she'd taken himself and Sasha to an old quarry mine simply to rescue a stray kitten she'd seen entering the dangerous zone. She'd been wild and adventur-ous and had really made him believe that one person, one voice, *could* make a difference in the world. Now…he'd upset her.

He opened his eyes and raked a hand through his hair. 'Nice going, Montgomery.' He walked around to his chair and sat, looking at the empty seat opposite him. Her scent still lingered in the air and the memory of how perfect she'd felt in his arms was potent. Just like before. Eden Caplan, the girl who had made him laugh, made him take a step out of his comfort zone, made him see her in a whole new light.

He knew it was inevitable that when a person grew up and had varying experiences in their life that it would change them. Sure, she still portrayed the same carefree Eden on the surface—but what was beneath the surface? A woman with scars? A woman who'd been through something that brought pain and anguish into her beautiful emerald-green eyes at the mere mention of it?

David stood and went to the bookshelf, pulling down the two volumes of paediatric journals he knew contained Eden's published papers.

He had no need to consult the index, flicking to the page almost automatically. He'd read the articles a few times and he'd been impressed and proud of her brilliance, glad she'd put that amazing intellect of hers to good use.

One of the papers was on the specialised care of underdeveloped children in an unsterilised environment, which he knew she'd encountered daily during her work overseas in Third World countries, but it was another article he wanted, about an unusual epidemic which had resulted in over twenty unexplained deaths. The paper cited the signs and symptoms as well as the probable causes. It was a well-formulated and well-written paper, giving information in the matter-of-fact way that was required for journal publications. Emotions weren't put on the page, but Eden had told him to read between the lines.

Although Eden was listed as the primary author of the paper, several of her colleagues' names appeared as well. He'd initially presumed she'd come across this information second-hand and decided to publish it for the common good, which was so typically Eden, but David now realised he'd been mistaken.

'She *lived* this.' The shocked words were whispered into the cold silence of his office. He read the article again, taking particular note of the statistics in which twenty children, ranging from one to seven years of age, had died before the cause of the epidemic had been discovered.

Eden had been the one trying to save those little lives. He knew it because he knew her. She would give and give and keep on giving everything she had to any cause other people classified as lost. She rooted for the underdog. She worked hard to lift the oppressed. Eden had been the one fighting for the lives of those children, and those twenty deaths would have weighed heavily on her heart.

The time she'd made him and Sasha help her look for the lost kitten in the quarry had shown him how closely she felt loss. They'd eventually found the kitten after dark, all of them using searchlights in a fenced-off area, but the poor animal had already died.

Eden hadn't said a word, but had lifted the creature and cradled it in her arms while they'd carried it back to her house. He'd dug a hole and they'd buried it in the backyard. She'd been solemn and sincere, saying a few brief words once he'd finished covering the small mound with dirt. Her younger brother Todd had found her grief funny, but that had been more due to his immature age than anything else.

Once the deed had been done, David and Sasha had left, but later that night he'd heard his sister on the phone, consoling a broken-hearted Eden, and he'd realised then just how deeply senseless loss affected the beautiful girl with the expressive eyes and gorgeous red hair.

Realising she'd witnessed the death of all those

children, been unable to 'fix' them, and no doubt been with the families when the small mounds had been covered, made tears spring to his eyes.

If this was the reason Eden hadn't made it back for Sasha's wedding then he *did* understand. Just as Sasha had. He also understood why Eden wouldn't want to discuss it. Something so deep, so tragic and unnecessary—and she would have taken it all on as her fault. As doctors, they all lost patients now and then, and they coped with that. They'd been trained to cope. But twenty children? All at once? All with the same signs and symptoms…with more to follow? His heart ached for Eden and the empathic pain he knew she would have experienced.

David shook his head, disgusted with himself for pushing her. He now had his answer and he knew he needed to apologise. It was also a relief to realise he hadn't misjudged her. Eden missing Sasha's wedding had surprised him, but he should have trusted her to have had a good reason. It did appear that in essentials Eden Caplan hadn't changed at all.

Clearing his throat, he closed the journals and returned them to the shelves, wondering what he could do to apologise for trampling on her emotions. Should he get her flowers? No. She didn't like cut flowers. A pot plant? No. She wouldn't be in town for long. He needed to think of something.

Perhaps a nice quiet dinner at one of her favourite hang-outs? That might be nice. Just the two of them. His eyes widened at the thought. He knew he'd vowed less than an hour ago to keep his distance where Eden was concerned, but his *faux pas* couldn't be left as it was. Besides, they were friends. Nothing more.

He could cope for one night.

Without stopping to think further on his idea, he decided to be impulsive and hauled out the phone book, quickly locating the number of a small Italian restaurant she'd frequented in her teens. He knew it was still there because every time he drove past it he would think of her and the way she'd slurped spaghetti until the sauce was all over her face. She would laugh brightly and encourage Sasha to do the same. David shook his head, remembering the way Eden had unlocked the gate of his sister's emotions. Sasha had been a girl who had been too shy to open up to anyone before Eden Caplan had entered their lives, filling it with laughter and sunshine.

He dialled the number and made reservations for that evening, knowing he could easily cancel them if she had other plans, although he secretly hoped she didn't. Once it was done, he realised that it was the first spontaneous thing he'd done in a long while. He'd always equated spontaneity with Eden, and here he was, back in her presence and already acting on impulse.

He laughed at himself. 'Really letting go, Montgomery. Dinner reservations? What a fly-by-the-seat-of-your-pants thing to do.'

Now all he had to do was to get Eden to agree to come. Would she?

Eden sat in the chair by the window, pretending to read a glossy magazine, but every so often her gaze flicked to Sasha, who was lying in bed, her eyes closed. Robert had gone to make a few phone calls, so it was just the two of them.

Eden was pleased she felt more in control. Thanks to David she'd been able to let go, to weep for her friend, and now she was ready to be strong, to get Sasha through the next few weeks at least. She flicked a page in the magazine, barely scanning it.

'Stop faking.' Sasha's weak words came from the bed. Eden looked at her but didn't move.

'Meaning?'

'You hate those glossy things. I remember you saying if women took the money they spent on shoes and put it towards a good charity instead, poverty in the world would be less and women wouldn't have so many painful calluses on their feet.'

Eden smiled. 'Well, it's true. I mean, just look at these shoes and the price they're asking for them.' She held up the page so Sasha could see. 'It's ridiculous.' She put the magazine down and walked towards the bed. 'I'm not saying people shouldn't buy shoes. Of course they need shoes to wear. But you can only wear one pair at a time.'

Sasha laughed. 'Same old Eden.'

'You sound like David—and enough with the old. You're the same age I am, missy.'

Sasha reached out her hand and Eden instantly took it. 'I know, but right now I feel ten times my age.'

'Rubbish.'

'Eden, it's true.' Sasha glanced behind her at the closed door. 'Where's Robert?'

'Gone to make some phone calls. He said he wouldn't be long. Do you want me to go find him?'

'No.' Sasha's word was insistent and her big brown eyes—which were so much like her brother's—stared at Eden. 'I'm scared, Ede.' Her lower lip began to quiver and her eyes instantly filled with tears. 'I've put on a brave face. I've told everyone not to cry, not to lie and not to look back, but…' She hiccuped. 'I can't walk. *I can't walk!*' The tears bubbled over. 'One minute my life is on track, and the next I'm lying in a hospital beneath a big round X-ray machine being told my spinal cord's been severely damaged and that I may never walk again. It's not fair. It's *so* not fair. Poor Robert looks at me like he doesn't know what to do next, and I don't know what I want him to do, and we've only been married for a few years and I love him so much, but it's not fair to put him through this, but if he leaves I'll just shrivel up into nothing, and I have to know… What am I supposed to do now?' She broke down and sobbed, clinging to Eden's arm.

Eden reached for a tissue with her free hand and gently dabbed the tears away, brushing the hair from her friend's face. The door to the private room opened and Eden glanced up as David slipped in. She silently communicated that he should stay back, which he did. Sasha's sobs were so heart-wrenching, so full of pain and despair it really was heartbreaking, but Eden was glad Sasha had finally broken down.

Softly she spoke. '*This* is what you're supposed to do, Sash. You're supposed to cry, honey. You're allowed to wallow, to feel sorry for yourself. You need to let the emotions out so the healing can come in.' She leaned closer and kissed Sasha's forehead. 'Don't be ashamed to cry.'

Sasha reached up with her other arm and hooked it around Eden's neck, holding her friend close as she cried. Eden could feel the pain, feel the anguish, and it was impossible to stop her own tears.

'I hate feeling sorry for myself,' Sasha whispered. 'What if I get so depressed I stay that way?'

'Not going to happen. You're too strong for that. Besides, a little depression is more than natural given what you've been through. You need to let it out, let out the stress and the anxiety and the uncertainty. You are surrounded by people who love you.'

Eden looked over at David and he walked towards his sister. Sasha looked up at him and David's heart constricted at the look in her eyes. It was as though she was six years old again and had done something wrong, and didn't have a clue what to do next.

'Cry, my sweet friend, because you'll feel much better—I promise.' Eden spoke softly but clearly near Sasha's ear. 'It's OK to cry. It's OK,' she soothed. 'I'm here, David's here, and let's not forget that brilliant husband of yours. We won't let you fall.' Eden sniffed as she spoke, her voice thick with emotion as she made such solemn promises to her friend. Tears slid down her cheeks as she felt Sasha's pain. Her tears must have landed on Sasha because her friend looked up.

'Why are *you* crying?' Sasha asked, sniffing and releasing her grip on Eden to reach for a tissue.

'Me? I'm not crying.' She wiped at her own eyes, belying her words. 'I merely have itchy eyes. On my way here I walked by the catering hall and they were chopping heaps of onions. I must have breathed in deeper than I thought and that's why my eyes are watering. Crying? *Pffttt!*' She waved the suggestion away as though it was ludicrous.

Sasha started laughing at the ridiculous excuse.

'That's our Eden. Isn't it, David? Always saying the craziest things.'

David looked across at Eden and acknowledged the deep, abiding friendship the two women had shared for most of their lives. For two weeks he'd watched his sister being brave, helping everyone else to deal with what had happened. He'd been deeply concerned that her own grieving process hadn't started, but now he realised she'd simply been waiting...waiting for Eden. Eden would be strong for Sasha, would help his sister through this difficult time.

What was *his* role, then? To be strong for Eden? To let her lean on him as she had just a few hours ago? The idea certainly had a definite appeal to it.

Eden smiled at her friend. 'It's what I'm here for. Now, take a deep breath. Nice and slow.' Sasha did as she was told. 'Then let it out just as slowly. There. Feel better?'

Sasha's answer was to look at her friend and laugh again. 'That's my Eden,' she repeated. 'You're such an amazing person.'

Eden dabbed gently at the corner of Sasha's eyes with a tissue. 'Right back at ya.'

'Ugh. I must look a sight.' Sasha tried to finger-comb her hair and Eden quickly found a brush and passed it over. David smiled at them.

'You both look like you've been chewing raw onions.'

'You're such a charmer, David Montgomery.'

'But you did eat raw onions once, right? I distinctly remember coming into the kitchen and you were both red-faced, puffy noses and eyes, and eating raw onions.'

Eden groaned. 'Do you remember every stupid thing we ever did?'

David grinned and crossed his arms over his chest, enjoying the opportunity to tease her a little. 'Pretty much. Why were you eating them again?'

Eden squared her shoulders. 'It was a test. To see if boys were stupid enough to do anything for a pretty girl, even if she smelled like onions.'

Sasha giggled. 'That's right. We had a dance on at school and three different boys had asked you to go. That was a funny night.'

The door to the room opened and this time it was Robert who came in. Sasha immediately put on a bright face, not wanting her husband to see she'd been upset. Eden gave her hand a squeeze and leaned down to whisper in her ear. 'Let him see you like this, Sash. Vulnerability is sometimes a good thing, and he loves you very much. Open up to him. Let him help you.' She kissed her friend's forehead again before pulling away.

Robert walked over to his wife's side and smiled down at her. 'You all right?'

'We've been eating onions.' Eden spoke matter-of-factly, as though the comment was perfectly normal. Sasha giggled when Robert looked blankly at her. 'I'll let Sash explain. David?' Eden smiled brightly at him and crossed to his side, lacing her arm through his and flicking her hair down her back. 'Why don't you show me your ward? I'd love to meet some of your patients.' She urged him towards the door and thankfully he picked up on her cue. 'I'll be back in about half an hour,' she said to Sasha over her shoulder.

'OK.' Sasha was looking lovingly at her husband.

'Eat some onions with Robert,' David suggested, before escorting Eden from the room.

Once they were out, Eden kept her arm where it was, even though she felt him shift away. 'They need to be alone.'

David agreed. 'It looks as though you've broken the drought.'

'Yes, thank goodness. Now hopefully they can cry together and heal together.'

David shook his head as they walked slowly along the corridor. 'You're quite a woman, Eden.'

'So glad you've noticed,' she said saucily. Since she'd discovered his parents had been the real reason why he'd left all those years ago, she felt as though at least one huge weight had been lifted from her shoulders. She tightened her grip on his arm, liking that she could be this close to him again.

David was well aware of the looks he was receiving from the nursing staff, and he smiled politely—as though it was more than natural for him to walk around the hospital with an incredible redhead on his arm.

'Eden. You're flirting again.'

'Am I, David? Well, thank you so much for pointing that out.'

'Perhaps you need to really eat some onions.'

'Would that stop you from holding my arm?'

'Who's holding whose arm?' he countered. He paused for a moment, then asked, 'Did it work?'

'Did what work?'

'The onion test. Did the *three* boys who

asked you to the dance do anything and everything for you?'

'Two did, one didn't. He was the one I dated.'

'How old were you?'

'Fifteen, I think. Yep. Bryce Martineau. Dated
him for a whole two weeks. But the chemistry
wasn't there so it was soon over.'

'Chemistry.' He muttered the word as he led
her into the stairwell. He didn't want to think
about physical chemistry when he was this close
to her.

'It's everything.'

'Hmm.' He'd hoped that in the stairwell she'd
let go of his arm, but instead she simply moved
closer and he knew exactly what she meant when
she said *chemistry*. Awareness was coursing
through him, the need to haul her into his arms and
press his mouth to hers was overwhelming and
difficult to resist, but resist, he would. 'Eden,
we're not going to fit up these stairs squashed
together.'

'No?' An imp of mischief buzzed through her
and she felt young and free, being with him,
being this close to him. He'd used to like it when
she was this close. In fact, she could recall plenty
of times when he'd crushed her into his arms,

holding her tightly as his mouth devoured hers. It had been the best time of her life so far, and a part of her wanted that throw-caution-to-the-wind feeling back again.

Her smile increased. 'Are you sure you don't want to try? Could be fun?' She wriggled a little, closing the distance, the side of her breast grazing against his chest.

David groaned and dropped her arm, moving right away from her—which was difficult given the confined space.

'Should have taken the lift,' he muttered, and she laughed, reaching down to take his hand.

'How about this? Is holding hands OK? After all, we are such dear old friends.' Without another word she tugged him forward, and he had little option but to follow her up the stairs. 'Now, which way to the ward?' she asked, not letting go of his hand.

He decided he might as well enjoy it for the moment, because he was only fooling himself if he denied the chemistry which coursed between them. It still didn't mean he was going to act upon it.

'Left.'

She turned left and soon they were at two big

doors which were painted with a bright and cheerful mural of animals, flowers and rainbows.

'Lovely. Your ward is just lovely, David.' She gave his hand a little squeeze before she let it go. 'Shall we?'

'We shall.' David opened the door, holding it for her like the gentleman he was.

'Ahh, there you are,' said one of the nurses, phone receiver in hand, as they walked to the nurses' station. Her badge said her name was Francie, and she replaced the phone. 'I was just about to page you.'

'What's the matter?'

'It's Dart.'

'Gone downhill?'

'Quite rapidly.'

'Is his mother here?'

Francie nodded. 'She arrived about an hour ago.'

'Did you tell her we were thinking of letting Dart go home tomorrow?'

'I did.'

David shook his head. 'Well, here's hoping we don't disappoint her. Has he had his medicine?'

Francie shook her head. 'He's refusing.'

All the time David had been discussing his patient with the nurse, Eden had been well aware of the interested glances she was receiving from the staff around them.

'Right. I'll go see what I can do. Oh, by the way, this is Eden. Eden Caplan.' David quickly introduced her. 'You may see her around during the next few weeks. There are some patients I'd like her to review.'

Eden raised her eyebrows at this news. She'd been quite happy just to play the role of visitor, but if David needed help...well, helping was what she did best.

CHAPTER THREE

'YOU need my help?'

'Yes.'

She winked at him and lowered her voice to a seductive whisper. 'I'm always happy to help out an old friend.'

Francie nearly choked on her tongue, and one of the other nurses stifled a giggle.

'Stop it.' David shook his head, a small smile twitching at his lips. 'Concentrate, Dr Caplan, and let's go take a look at Dart.'

'Dart?' Eden was all business and efficiency as she followed David to the first bay of beds. Francie was behind her.

'Short for d'Artagnan.'

'Really? That's going to turn a few heads when he gets older. What's the situation?'

'The poor boy is up and down like a yo-yo. Dehydration, stomach pain, headaches, dizziness. He's been scanned, poked, prodded and still I can't figure it out.'

'Multiple admissions?'

'This is his second with these symptoms.' David pulled back the curtain which was around Dart's bed. Mrs Wilman quickly stood from where she'd been sitting on the bed next to her son. She held a child's drinking cup in her hands as though she were trying to persuade her son to keep his fluids up. She quickly put the cup on the bedside table.

'Hey there, Dart,' said David, smiling a greeting at the mother. 'I hear you're not feeling as well as you were this morning.'

'I'm afraid he's not well at all, Dr Montgomery.' Mrs Wilman was earnest in her words. 'I don't understand what you've done to him. You were supposed to be making him better.'

'He'd improved dramatically overnight. Earlier this morning he was bouncing around on his bed and running about the ward.'

'He quite clearly should have been lying still and resting.' Mrs Wilman's tone was more one of stress rather than accusing the staff of neglect. 'Now I'm sorry I didn't stay last night with Dart. He was probably so distraught at my leaving him that he's had a relapse. I don't think sending him home is at all a wise move. Do you, Dr Montgomery?' She shook her head as she spoke, and before David could answer continued. 'I think he'll need to stay for at least another few days—if not the week.'

David held out his hand for a stethoscope, and Francie had one at the ready. 'Hey, Dart. Can I have a listen to your chest and your tummy, please?' He pulled the covers down and smiled reassuringly at the four-year-old.

Eden was busy watching. Not only what David was doing, but also keeping a close eye on the mother. Mrs Wilman was obviously very upset and concerned about her son, but there was something else going on. Eden had no idea what—it was just a hunch, and in the past she'd learned to follow those hunches.

'It hurts,' Dart moaned, and David nodded.

'I know, mate. Let's see if we can't get you better.'

'I don't want the yucky meddy.'

'I know,' he said again, before continuing with his examination. When he palpated Dart's stomach, the little boy groaned.

'You need to get him back to Radiology for

another scan of his abdomen.' Mrs Wilman was quite insistent as she spoke to David. 'I really think this time, Dr Montgomery, that an MRI should be requested. In fact, I'm quite insistent about it.'

'Hmm.' David was half listening to what Dart's mother was saying, but was far more concerned with trying to figure out why the little boy had gone downhill so quickly. He looked at Mrs Wilman. 'I'd like to put Dart back on an IV drip, and I'll order some more tests. I'm not convinced at this point whether an MRI scan is necessary, but it's certainly something to consider down the track.'

'I'm not completely satisfied with that diagnosis, Dr Montgomery,' Mrs Wilman counteracted. 'I'm certain an MRI is the next step in my son's treatment, and if you *don't* order one I'll get someone else to order the tests. I'll go above your head if necessary. I don't want to, but I will.'

'I'm head of the paediatric department at St Thomas' hospital. When it comes to the treatment of children, no one is more qualified than myself. You are, however, more than welcome to a second opinion.' David indicated Eden. 'For instance, Dr Caplan here is a trained paediatrician who has worked extensively overseas. She is widely published on topics which include mysterious illness in children, and is highly regarded by her peers. I've already asked her for her valued opinion on Dart's condition, because I can assure you, Mrs Wilman, I am just as concerned as you are about his health.'

Mrs Wilman looked at Eden, giving her the once-over before turning her attention back to David. 'Well, I'm pleased to see you're doing *something* to try and fix my son.' She looked to Eden. 'I hope you have some new ideas, or at least can persuade Dr Montgomery to see sense by advising him to order an MRI.'

Eden smiled warmly at the woman, who seemed to know quite a bit about medical procedures and terminology. 'I must say it's so nice to see a parent such as yourself taking an interest in their child's health.'

Mrs Wilman straightened her cardigan. 'What mother wouldn't?'

'Oh, believe me, there are plenty. As Dr Montgomery said, I've been working overseas in areas where a lot of parents are so busy trying to find work that they can't afford to spend time looking after their sick children. It's fantastic that you're here for Dart and that you're willing to get really involved, to question and seek out different answers. So many parents are so…lax at times.'

'I see.' Mrs Wilman almost preened. 'Well, you'll find that I'm not one of *those* types of parents. I do know exactly the sort of parent you're talking about, though. So many of my… acquaintances are more concerned with their careers rather than what's most important in their lives.' She looked down at her son. 'That's why I'm here for d'Artagnan. It's why I stay at the hospital overnight. Last night was the first night I wasn't able to be here, and look what has happened today upon my return.' She reached out and stroked the hair from her son's forehead.

David's tone was firm. 'Francie, would you do observations again? Let me know if there has been any change. Get the IV line in whilst I have a chat with Eden.' He looked at Dart's mother. 'We'll get him sorted out.'

After they'd returned to the nurses' station, Eden shook her head. 'What?' David asked, clearly agitated that he couldn't figure out what was happening with his little patient.

'You shouldn't promise like that.'

'I know, but I want to figure this out. I'm really worried about him. The thing is that his reaction to the usual medicine is that it seems to work initially, and then, *wham*, something happens and he goes downhill again.'

'So we just need to figure out what the "wham" part is, eh?'

'Exactly.' David shook his head and lowered his voice. 'Any help you can offer would be gratefully received. Have you ever seen anything like it?'

'Hand me his notes. Let me review them and we'll see what we can come up with.' David did as she asked and she took the notes, meeting his gaze. 'We'll find out…together.'

David swallowed at her words, and seeing the look in her eyes, wondered how she could make one little word sound so intimate. 'Uh…right. Yes. Together.'

A smile touched her lips. 'I like you most when you're flustered.'

'Hmm. Well. Er…' He cleared his throat. 'Listen, whilst you're here in the hospital I'll organise for you to receive Visiting Medical Officer status. That will make things a bit more aboveboard—especially as Mrs Wilman seems to be shopping for my scalp.'

Eden nodded. 'She is a little gung-ho. It's good to see that she's taking an interest in her son, that she's here with him, but she needs to trust you more. You are the one with the medical degrees, after all.'

'A lot of parents freak out when their children are ill. Mrs Wilman's actually quite nice. She's helpful to the staff, and encouraging with other parents who are here—showing them where the tea and coffee facilities are, that sort of thing.'

'OK. Let me get through these notes. I hope you don't mind if I ask the nurses some questions as well?'

'Investigating me?' He raised an eyebrow.

'Investigating Dart.' Eden smiled at him, seeing his veiled concern. Had he forgotten that she knew him so well? 'Sometimes you need to think outside the box. You might be a little too close to the situation, holding on a little too tightly.'

'Is that what you've learnt overseas? To see things differently? To try different approaches?'

'You have to. We don't have access to most of the facilities you have at your fingertips. We have to improvise, to think of alternatives, to see beyond the normal way of things.'

'You sound as though you enjoy it very much.'

'I do.' Eden sighed. 'Although sometimes…' She looked away from him, down at Dart's notes. 'Sometimes it gets a little draining. Even *I've* been too close to a project before. Needed someone to come along and point out the simplest of solutions. It happens to all of us.'

Was she referring to the epidemic he'd read about in the journal? When he'd asked her for assistance he hadn't wanted to raise any old ghosts, to awaken any old memories. That hadn't been his intention. He'd merely been after a fresh perspective. He didn't want to hurt her. 'Listen, Eden. If you'd rather not help me out—if you just want to relax and spend time with Sasha—then I—'

Eden reached across the desk to where he was sitting, placing a finger over his lips. 'Shh. That wasn't what I meant. You know I'll always help you. You're my friend, David, and friends help each other.' Her words had slowed as she realised just what she'd done, just how close they were…*again*.

David's expressive brown eyes had widened at her touch, and now she watched as his gaze dipped to her lips, lingering briefly before rising to meet her eyes once more. Eden's breathing slowly started to increase, and she wished the world would simply freeze so she could figure out exactly what it was that existed between herself and David.

Sure, they were attracted to each other. Sure, they had a bit of history together. Sure, they'd both changed over the past decade. Life, however, didn't always turn out the way you planned. She quickly dropped her hand back to her side. 'Besides…' She tapped Dart's case notes and forced an overly bright smile to try and cover up the devastating effect he was having on her equilibrium. 'I'm intrigued. Go. Do what you need to do and let me review.'

David opened his mouth to speak, but no words came out. He closed it quickly, nodded, and then walked back to his office. There were a few other patients he wanted her to meet, especially the eleven-year-old girl who had been admitted with anorexia, but that could wait. He headed back to his office and tapped a few commands into his computer to bring up the template for the forms he needed to fill in. The idea of making Eden a VMO wasn't what he'd initially had in mind, but seeing how she'd managed to win Mrs Wilman over in a matter of seconds was enough of an impetus for David to forge ahead.

He sent the form to print, then sat back in his chair and closed his eyes. Why had she touched him like that? The imprint of her finger was still on his lips. The warmth, the tenderness, the… *Eden*-ness…it was all still there. He licked his lips, and the hunger he'd been trying to control from the first instant he'd laid eyes on her that morning started to burn harder and faster than before.

Memories of the times they'd spent together came instantly to mind, and he knew for certain that if he kissed her again his world would once again be rocked on its foundations. He couldn't have that. She had been the first girl he'd dated who he'd been serious about. He'd enjoyed her company, been amazed by her intelligence and had valued her opinion. Those factors alone had been enough for his parents to ship him off to Melbourne, away from Eden. Even though he now had little to do with his parents, he knew that the effect Eden still had on him was as strong as it had been back then. He couldn't even risk getting involved with her because she meant far too much to him. She meant far too much to Sasha, and his sister had already been through enough.

If Eden ever found out about his accident, discovered his own dark secret, then he would be diminished in her view. Just as he had been in Jacquie's. When his ex-wife had realised the truth, that David could never father children, she'd started seriously discussing divorce. As far as she had been concerned there had been no reason to continue in the marriage. Things had already been strained, and both had agreed their friendship was the one thing worth salvaging from their incompatible marriage.

For some reason Eden's opinion of him mattered far more than he'd realised, but perhaps it was because she'd looked up to him for so long, for so many years. They had a past, a history which was more than just the chemistry between them. They'd been friends, and if he couldn't have anything else with her, friendship would be the next best thing.

The phone on his desk rang and he instantly snatched it up, relieved to have something to ponder other than Eden Caplan.

There was nothing untoward in the case notes, and Eden was now as perplexed as David. She'd spoken with Francie, and some of the other nurses who had cared for Dart during his admission, but still nothing obvious seemed to jump out at her.

She'd been in to see Dart, to do some observations of her own and try and talk to him, but he'd just lain on his bed, listless and depressed. Something was really wrong in this little boy's world, and she wasn't sure it was all physical. Psychological issues could make a person very sick indeed.

'Four-year-olds don't get depressed,' one of the nurses said.

'Yes, they do. All the time,' Eden remarked. 'I've seen a lot of children depressed for quite long lengths of time. Children younger than four as well.'

'That must have been heartbreaking.' Francie had already pumped Eden for information about the various countries Eden had worked in, as well as on what it was like working for a medical aid organisation.

'I've been through worse. Of course a lot of the time the children don't *realise* it's depression. Things are bad. There's no way they can get better and they slump down, their spirits crushed.

Thankfully, though, it doesn't take much to buoy them up again. Children are far more resilient than adults.'

'So we need to find a way to boost Dart's spirits?'

'Until we can figure out what's causing his relapse, why not?'

'Were you successful with the IV line?' David spoke from behind Francie and the nurse jumped.

'Good golly, Miss Molly. You're so quiet, I didn't even hear you there. The IV line is in. He just lay there. No fuss at all.'

David frowned. 'This is perplexing. Eden?'

'I've got nothing. Apart from the blood tests you've ordered and the medication you have him on, I can't think of anything I'd do differently.'

'Do you think it's worth doing the MRI?'

Eden pondered this for a moment. 'I'm not sure it's going to give you any new information after the scans Dart's already had. The only thing it will do is appease the mother, and that's a very expensive way to appease her.'

'Hmm.' David was pensive once more.

'You know what? Perhaps a change of scenery might help.'

'Meaning?'

'I'm going to go see your sister. Want to join me?'

David hesitated for a moment. More time alone with Eden? He wasn't sure he could handle so much in one day. Then again, he *had* made dinner reservations for them—but that was different. That was his way of apologising for being an insensitive clod, and that apology still needed to be made. Besides, at dinner they'd be in a crowded restaurant. They'd be eating and enjoying polite conversation.

He'd already been alone with her in a hospital stairwell today and look what had happened. She'd flirted with him, and the fact that he'd liked it was completely beside the point. As a man wanting to keep his distance from a woman he wasn't doing a very good job—and he wasn't the sort of man to enjoy conflict within himself.

'Go see your sister,' Francie chimed in when he didn't say anything. It was then David realised that Eden had stood and was ready to go. 'I'll call you immediately if there's any change with Dart.'

'OK.' He looked at Eden. 'Let's go.'

This time as they walked between the two wards Eden didn't attempt to take his hand, touch him or flirt with him in any way, shape or form.

'Are you all right?' he eventually asked.

'Sure. I'm fine. Just pondering things.'

'What are you going to do once you've seen Sasha?'

'Why? How many patients have you got for me to review? Or were you just saying that to appease me? To stop me from being bored whilst I'm back in town?'

'Uh…no. I really do have a few more cases I'd like your opinion on.'

'My cases have been vastly different from the ones you usually have here,' she felt compelled to point out.

'That's what I mean. I'm counting on your unique perspective—your Eden way of thinking things through.'

'My "Eden way" of thinking?' She turned and smiled at him, and it was then he realised that she looked tired. Very tired, in fact. Not in essentials, but just about her eyes. A passer-by wouldn't notice anything amiss, but he did. He knew her too well.

'When did you arrive back in Australia?'

'Eight o'clock this morning. My room wasn't

ready when I checked into my hotel, so I left my luggage there and headed straight here. I needed to see Sasha, to see for myself that she was OK, even though she'd assured me several times on the phone. However, I'm starting to feel a little worn out now.' She flicked her skirt with her hand. 'And I think a change of clothes is definitely in order. I feel as though I've been wearing this outfit for ever.' She grinned. 'And I have!'

How was it possible? he wondered as they stopped outside Sasha's door. She still looked fresh and bright, and now she was telling him she'd just travelled halfway round the world. That was impossible. No one could look this good after travelling all night and then spending the morning in a hospital. David's gaze encompassed her again, taking in her leather sandals, long flowing skirt and matching top. He was glad she'd left her hair loose. It was quite a bit longer than it had been the last time he'd seen her. He liked it.

As though his hand had a mind of its own, he reached out and tenderly took a handful of the rich auburn tresses. Eden didn't smile, but her gaze remained riveted on his as he sifted the strands through his fingers.

'The colour's slightly darker,' he murmured, and she tried not to gasp at the huskiness in his tone.

The attraction she'd felt for him in the past had developed slowly. First he'd just been Sasha's big brother, then he'd been someone she'd thought was cute, then someone she'd listened to, and then someone whose opinion she'd valued. Finally she'd become aware of the growing attraction which had existed between them and which had eventually led to them dating. What she hadn't expected now was for the attraction to be stronger than ever, to have actually increased since she'd first seen him that morning.

The breath she'd been unconsciously holding escaped her lips at his touch. Then, as though he'd realised what he was doing, he quickly dropped his hand and cleared his throat. 'You…er…don't look unkempt, if that's what you're worried about.'

Eden shrugged, temporarily unable to speak as she tried to get her emotions under control. She was tongue-tied and glued to the spot simply because David had voluntarily touched her hair. Even though the touch had been brief, it had been tantalising—sensual, and a complete breach of her comfort zone, but one she was more than willing to allow. She put her current state of mind down to too much emotional turmoil and not enough sleep.

'Eden…er…do you have any plans for dinner this evening?'

She looked at him a little perplexed. Out of everything he could have said, that wasn't what she'd expected. She'd thought he wouldn't want to spend any more time with her than was necessary, given that by touching her hair in such an intimate way he'd openly acknowledged the attraction, the chemistry which existed between them. Then again, perhaps David had just asked because it was the right thing to do—and David always did the right thing.

She swallowed. 'Ah…no. I was going to see how Sasha was doing, but I think it's best if she and Robert have some more time together tonight. Besides, my day is starting to catch up with me.'

He nodded, understanding that she was tired. 'That's OK. If you're tired, we don't have to go. It's no problem.'

Go? Was he asking her out? 'No. I didn't mean it like that.' She spoke quickly. 'I don't have any plans and I'd love to have dinner with you tonight…if that is what you're asking.'

His smile was gorgeous as he spoke. 'Obviously I'm doing a very poor job. I guess it's been a while since I've asked a woman to dinner.'

'Well, if it helps, it's been a while since I've accepted. Just tell me where you want to meet and when and I'll be there. I can't say for sure what type of company I'll be, but hopefully I'll have managed to sneak in a bit of a nap before night-time hits, so I'll be bright-eyed and bushy-tailed.'

'We have reservations for seven. Is that too early? Too late?'

Eden was touched. Excitement coursed through her at knowing that David had already made plans. It made her feel special, pretty and feminine, and she hadn't felt like that in…she couldn't remember when. David wanted to take her to dinner. She didn't care why because right now just the thought was all she needed to make her happy.

'Seven sounds great.'

'OK. I'll meet you at your hotel.'

'Perfect. Thank you so much for thinking of it.' Stepping forward, she wrapped her arms about his neck and hugged him close. 'A nice quiet dinner with you is just what I need,' she said softly near his ear.

David was surprised at the embrace, but he should have expected it. It was so Eden. He withdrew his hands from his pockets and placed them gently at her waist, easing her back slightly so her gorgeous body wasn't pressed so firmly against his. She must have felt his restraint because she instantly pulled back.

'Perfect,' she repeated, feeling more relaxed and more herself. 'Shall we go and see Sash?'

David cleared his throat. 'Why don't you go in? I'll catch up with her later on in the day. I want to get your VMO paperwork rushed through.'

'Oh. OK, then. Well, I guess I'll see you tonight at seven.' She quickly gave him the name of her hotel before she forgot, then pushed open Sasha's private room door and went inside with a beaming smile on her face.

David walked into the lobby of the hotel, surprised at the apprehension in the pit of his stomach. What was there to be apprehensive about? It was just Eden. He walked over to the Guest Services desk and asked them to call her room. While he waited, he recalled a good many reasons why he should be apprehensive about Eden—and number one was the undeniable attraction he felt for her.

It didn't seem to matter how many lectures he gave himself, determining to keep his distance, to keep whatever contact he had with her down to a minimum and make sure that contact was light and friendly. That was what he was planning to do tonight. Light and friendly.

Then he saw her.

He was positive his jaw went slack at the sight she made, walking across the lobby towards him with that sexy swish of her hips. She was dressed in another flowing creation, although this time it was a dress rather than a skirt and top. It came to just above her knees, revealing far too much leg for his liking. Her shape was perfect—nice and curvy, the way a woman should be. She was a bombshell with the most gorgeous hair, her auburn curls flowing loosely around her shoulders, clipped back on one side with a frangipani blossom.

'Hi.' She came to stand before him, her perfume making it difficult for him to think rationally.

'What are you wearing?' They were the first words out of his mouth, and he wished them unsaid the next moment. His tone held a hint of censure, of that big-brother protectiveness he'd often used on Sasha and Eden when they'd been younger.

Eden's response was to torture him further by doing a slow twirl. 'Do you like it?'

David couldn't help but look at her as she showed off her delectable body. His heart was pounding wildly at the intoxicating sight she made and he shifted awkwardly.

'I bought it this afternoon. I must say it feels so soft against my skin. Almost melts into it.' Eden watched David's reaction closely, loving the way he seemed stuck for words, his Adam's apple working its way up and down his gorgeous throat as he swallowed nervously. She lowered her tone a notch and leaned a little closer. 'I was thinking of you when I bought it.'

David straightened the lapels of his jacket and cleared his throat. 'Right. Well. We should…go.'

'Sure.'

'Do you have a jacket?' Something ankle-length, which would hide her body from everyone else. David glanced around the lobby for a second, noting there were several appreciative glances being sent her way. 'Or have you forgotten what Sydney is like in early spring?'

Eden's answer was to indicate the shawl she had draped over her arm. She went to open it and David quickly helped her, taking it abruptly from her hands before placing it around her shoulders. He hadn't even realised she'd been holding it, along with a small clutch purse, because he'd obviously been too distracted by the rest of her.

'I haven't forgotten what Sydney weather is like, but my body is acclimatised to Ukrainian weather and it's a tad colder there—especially in winter. It's also why I went and bought a new dress. I never get the time to dress up and go out, so this is definitely a special occasion.' She linked her arm through his, then leaned up and pressed a small, light kiss to his cheek. 'Thank you for asking me out tonight.' Her tone was one hundred percent sincere, and he found that side of Eden even more difficult to resist.

David simply stood there, looking down at her, at this gorgeous woman who had been through so much in her life yet continued to persevere. He could see the pain hidden deep beneath her hypnotic green eyes, which were now highlighted with the skilful application of mascara and eyeshadow, making her even more stunning than usual.

Eden didn't move. Didn't want to move. David was looking at her in such a way that she wasn't at all sure what would happen next. She was sure if she leaned over to give him a kiss that they might end up changing their plans. If she'd had any doubts about whether or not he was attracted to her, they vanished into thin air.

It had been her main purpose when she'd stumbled across the dress hanging in a shop window that afternoon as she'd walked from the hospital to her hotel. To see whether she could knock his socks off. She was pleased that she'd succeeded. However, they couldn't spend the rest of the night standing in the hotel lobby, gazing into each other's eyes.

'Shall we go?' The words were a whisper from her lips, and it took a split second for them to penetrate David's hazy mind. He looked down at her lips one more time, and Eden held her breath, waiting to see what would happen.

Then he looked away, the moment broken. 'Of course.'

As they headed out into the early evening, Eden's excitement start to increase. She was out on a date, with David. Well, he might not call it a date, but she most certainly did. She'd dreamed about this—the two of them going out to dinner—so many years ago, her seventeen-year-old heart desperate for some grown-up time with him rather than eating pizza and studying. Now that it was actually happening she was pleased they hadn't done it before, because it made tonight more special.

'I wasn't sure whether you wanted to take the car or walk.' His voice was a little clipped as he desperately tried not to breathe in her scent, but he knew he was fighting a losing battle. Eden was alluring, and he was beginning to realise just how addictive she was. He named the restaurant and Eden racked her brain trying to remember where it was. 'It's two blocks away. Not far.'

She nodded. 'That's right. All I remember is the food. Delicious, and exactly what I'm in the mood for.'

'Walk?'

'Absolutely.' She tightened her hold on his arm. 'At least that way I get to be closer to you for longer.' She waggled her eyebrows up and down. David didn't comment, but merely smiled politely. 'Add to that fact you can help support me in these shoes. I am definitely not used to wearing high heels.'

David chuckled at this information.

'What's so funny?'

'You. You breeze into the lobby as though you're so sure of yourself, turning everyone's head, portraying a woman who is as stable as she is sexy, and then you go and confess you're not as confident as you appear.'

'Well, *you* try walking in these things. They're not too bad in the comfort department, but it's early on. Who knows? By the time the night is over you might be giving me a piggy-back all the way home.'

David grinned at the image this produced. 'Why are you wearing them, then?'

'Because they go perfectly with the dress. They complete the picture.' She spoke as though he'd asked the most ridiculous question possible.

'Right. That explains it all.'

'Ahh…you may feign nonchalance now, but your look back at the hotel told me otherwise.'

'What look?' David kept his eyes straight ahead, knowing that if he looked at the woman beside him she would see far too much. So much for guarding himself around her.

'The one that said you wanted to devour me.'

David was stunned. Had he been so transparent? He closed his eyes for a brief second, his mind working frantically as he tried to decide the best course of action. He eventually decided upon humour. Keep it light and friendly.

'You're trying to razz me up again, aren't you?'

'Is it working?'

He glanced down at her, their gazes melding. 'I'm already razzed.' The soft words were out before he could stop them. He saw surprise and then total appreciation in her eyes.

'And you're *admitting* this to me?'

David exhaled slowly. 'It seems pointless not to. All day long I've struggled against the way you make me feel. It's there. It exists between us. Is there any point in denying it?'

'No. *No.*' Eden was astonished. 'Not at all. This new, not-afraid-to-admit-his-feelings David is a delightful find.'

'It doesn't matter, because we both know nothing can ever come of it.'

'Why?'

'You don't live in this country, Eden. You work overseas, and we've been a wrong fit right from the start. You forget that I know you better than the plethora of men you usually play with.'

'Play with?' She quirked an eyebrow at him, trying to hide the way his words were making her feel. First elation, then excitement, then dejection.

'There will have been plenty of men over the years—none of them serious, though. Am I right?'

Eden considered his words carefully before answering. 'Not entirely.'

'Some serious, then?' A surge of jealousy instantly coursed through him, catching him completely off guard. The picture of Eden with her arms wrapped around another man, pressing her body, her full, delicious mouth to his, was more than David could bear. He blinked fiercely, the vision dissipating.

'Not as such. Just not as many men as you're referring to. You forget I've been working overseas in remote areas for the past few years. Not a lot of socialising goes on.'

'All work and no play?' Now, why had her words made him feel happier?

'Exactly. Hence the need to dress up and enjoy myself tonight.' They stopped at a red light and she looked up at him, wondering just how far she could razz him. 'Besides, there was this guy I dated when I was seventeen, and he kind of set the bar as far as men were concerned.'

David cleared his throat and swallowed nervously. 'Is that so?'

'That is most definitely so. You rocked my world back then, David.'

He swallowed again, and forced himself to look away from her mesmerising eyes. 'Light's green,' he choked out, and was rewarded with a little chuckle from the woman beside him—the woman who could still tie him in knots with just a few words.

The restaurant was only a few doors past the crossing, and soon they were seated at an intimate table. The candlelight reflecting off her hair almost gave her a halo effect. Eden? A halo? He smiled at the idea. Sure, she fought for worthy causes, righted wrongs and generally supported the underdog—but a *halo*? Then he remembered what she'd been through a few years ago and the main reason why he'd decided to take her out to dinner. Perhaps she did deserve that halo after all.

Once they'd ordered, David raised his glass of wine to her. 'To new beginnings,' he said, and tapped his glass gently with hers.

'Are you talking about you and me?' Her curls bounced softly around her, and he couldn't believe how incredibly beautiful she was.

He nodded.

'Do we *need* a new beginning?' she asked. 'Because I like the one we already have.'

He thought for a moment. 'So do I. However, I was referring to the way I annoyed you earlier today.'

'You didn't annoy me, David. You excite and confuse me, but you don't annoy me.'

He groaned. 'Don't say things like that when I'm trying to apologise.'

'Apologise? For what?'

'For pressuring you to tell me why you didn't make it to Sasha's wedding.'

'Oh.' Eden looked down at her glass for a moment, before meeting that rich, chocolate gaze of his once more. He was so handsome, and just being here, sitting opposite him, made her heart pound wildly against her ribs. 'You didn't pressure me. Well, not much—and it's all right. I understand that you were confused. After all, Sasha and I are so very close. She's the only person who's ever really cared about me.'

That wasn't true. *He* certainly cared about her, but telling her might only bring them closer and he was trying to make sure there was distance between them. 'I read your articles. I read between the lines.' David reached across the table and took her free hand in his. 'Eden. I'm sorry.'

Eden looked down at their entwined fingers, a lump forming in her throat. She'd resigned herself years ago to the tragedy which had occurred. She'd had counselling, she'd worked through her emotions, and yet now, with David displaying such honest tenderness, all the helplessness she'd felt back then surged to the forefront.

'They were so small. Tiny, undernourished children. Disgusting living conditions and disease at every turn.' She raised her eyes slowly, meeting his. 'It was horrible, David. Their pain, their suffering. It was there in their big wide eyes. Those looks still haunt me. They looked to me to help them, to make them better.' She pursed her lips together to try and control her emotions. closing her eyes. 'I couldn't. The sounds of mothers wailing as their children were taken from them. The lifelessness of those little bodies—bodies I had held in my arms, willing them to hold on, praying for a miracle. The smell of death in the air, the breaking of hearts, the utter desolation.'

A tear slid down her cheek, but she made no

attempt to wipe it away. 'On a day that was supposed to be so important to me—the day my best friend got married—I was attending a mass funeral instead.'

'Eden.' David tightened his grip on her hand and leaned over to brush the tear from her cheek with his thumb.

Her eyes snapped open and she pulled back from his touch as though burnt. Letting go of his hand, she clasped hers together, dragging in a cleansing breath.

'Sasha wanted to postpone her wedding until I could be there, but I had no idea when that might be so I encouraged her to proceed without me. I needed to know that at least *she* was happy. You have no idea how much comfort that thought gave me in those dark days. My Sasha. Happily married to a man who adores her.' Eden blinked again. 'Anyway, if you'll excuse me?' She stood from the table, taking her purse with her. 'Won't be long.'

David watched her go, feeling almost as drained as she had looked. He'd been moved by her words, astonished that she'd opened up, that she'd shared with him, and yet at the same time he wanted her to stop torturing herself by reliving it yet again. How many times had she done that?

Spoken about that dark time? She'd written about it in a medical journal, sharing the facts of what had happened in an analytical fashion. She'd no doubt been treated by a therapist. And yet despite the passage of time, and the fact that she and her team had eventually discovered a cure, he knew she felt each and every one of those deaths every day. He knew that because he knew Eden.

She might come across as flirty and thriving, but there was another side to her, a deeper side— far deeper than he'd previously realised. When she'd spoken of Sasha being adored by Robert there had been a wistfulness in her tone.

Ever since he'd first met her she'd been this person with so much energy. Helping others. Giving everything of herself. It was no wonder she'd ended up in the career she now had. He'd always thought that that satisfied her, that helping others was enough, but in her vulnerability she'd shown him something else.

She'd shown him that she wanted more. In fact, she wanted the fairytale. She wanted to find that special someone—that man who would love, cherish and adore her. The man who would understand her need to help others and yet provide the help that *she* needed. Sasha had found that with Robert, and Eden envied that.

David's heart stirred as he watched her walk back towards him, her body swaying in such a provocative way. He wasn't sure she was conscious of how incredible she looked. A surge of protectiveness flooded through him for the second time that day, but this time it wasn't the protective instinct of a brother-sister relationship.

This was the protectiveness of a man who was falling in love with a woman.

CHAPTER FOUR

THE instant the revelation hit, he emphatically denied it.

It was completely and utterly impossible that he was in love with Eden. She was like a sister to him and the feelings he felt were purely those of a big brother. Although a tiny voice said this was totally different from the way he felt about Sasha.

He'd just seen too much of her today. It was like an Eden overdose, which had brought back so many memories of when he'd been younger. Even back then he'd had trouble keeping his feelings for her under control, preferring instead to focus on the long slog of medical school which had been before him. That wasn't the case now. Sure, he had a high-powered, pressured job, but he was well trained and knew how to control his stress. He'd succeeded in so many of his goals, and yet in others he would never succeed. He would never be a father.

Yes, he was attracted to Eden. He admitted that. But it was the fact that he cared for her so much in a brotherly way and he didn't want to see her hurt. He knew if he let things get out of hand that he would indeed hurt her. She was a woman made to be the mother of a gaggle of her own children—little imps with wild curls and cheeky green eyes.

He could never give her that.

He could, however, help her to be strong for Sasha. He could even help her to heal the rift she had with her family. He would do everything he could to make her happy, to make sure the pain and vulnerability which remained behind her eyes was protected. He could do all of this as a platonic friend. He could help her help herself. Deep down inside she appeared to be lost, and he could help her find herself.

'Now,' she said as she sat back down at the table, an overly bright smile on her face, 'let the feast begin.'

'You've certainly ordered enough food.' He took a sip of his wine, pleased he had a more logical footing on his thoughts.

'You're not being a tight date, are you David?' She tut-tutted. 'After all these years we finally make it out to dinner, and you're complaining about the cost.'

He gulped on the mouthful of wine, swallowing too quickly. 'I am not a "tight date", as you so eloquently term it, nor am I complaining about the cost. I was merely stating the fact that you've ordered a lot of food for someone so small.'

'Ahh, I may only be five feet six—which is no doubt short compared to your over-six-foot, muscled and well-toned frame—but I'll have you know in some countries I'm considered tall.'

He smiled at that. 'Really?'

'Don't sound so surprised—and besides, I'm counting on you to help me eat the mountain of food that's coming. It's been ages since I've eaten here…well, eaten at any restaurant for that matter…and I intend to thoroughly enjoy myself.'

The smile was back—the true smile of Eden—and David relaxed. Platonic friends. Good company. Flirty banter. He could deal with that. So long as he kept his hands by his sides and didn't touch her.

When their first course arrived, David watched as she lovingly savoured every mouthful. Again and again she showed her appreciation and delight for the food as they continued to talk about a variety of topics. 'Mmm…delicious,' she declared again as she slurped her spaghetti, a drop of the sauce landing on the side of her mouth.

David looked at it. Couldn't help but focus on it. And he wasn't at all surprised at the powerful urge to lean over and kiss it away. She had the most luscious lips, full and inviting, and sitting opposite her, breathing in her scent, he was starting to lose his will-power.

'David?'

He dragged his gaze back up to meet hers, realising he'd been staring at her.

'Hmm? Sorry? What were you saying?'

Eden took a mouthful from her water glass and swallowed, letting her thoughts calm for a moment. David had been looking at her as though he wanted to toss the table and all its contents aside, scoop her into his arms and devour her one inch at a time. It was heady stuff.

She'd been surprised earlier when he'd admitted that she razzed him up—that she, in essence, got his blood pumping—but to see him gazing upon her in this way was almost too much for her to ignore. She might be tired, exhausted and starting to feel the initial effects of jet lag, but that wouldn't stop her from encouraging him…if he intended to actually do something about it.

This was *David*. The man responsible for her first real love. It was a love which had been growing and festering with the passing years. It was quite true that he was the man she measured all others by, but could it be that her feelings for him were far deeper than she'd previously thought?

'You shouldn't look at me like that.' Her tone was soft, barely a whisper, but he heard it. In fact, he *felt* her words more than heard them, such was the connection between them.

He cleared his throat, shifting in his seat, feeling highly self-conscious. 'Er…like what? How am I looking at you?'

'As though you still want to devour me.' She blinked slowly, then leaned forward onto her elbows. 'It's all right, you know. I don't mind.'

'Eden!'

The bubble which had encapsulated them burst, and she couldn't help but laugh sweetly at the expression on his face. It held a mixture of disbelief, doubt and desire.

'You're not supposed to say those sorts of

things to a man. Is this how you usually conduct your dates?'

'Ahh…so you're admitting this is a date? Interesting.'

'It's dinner. Between friends.'

'That look you just gave me said you'd like to be *very* friendly.' She was deadly serious in what she was saying, but kept her tone light, jovial. If he thought she was just teasing, perhaps she'd be able to get more out of him. With all she knew about him, for all the history they shared, he was still a difficult man to read—especially when it came to affairs of the heart.

David took a deep breath in and let it out slowly, deciding the best way to calm things down was to be honest with her. 'Eden, I'm not a blind fool who doesn't recognise the attraction, the tension which exists between us. Of course I find you attractive, but I also admire and respect you far too much to think of changing the strong friendship we currently have. You have your life. I have mine. Our paths have crossed again because of Sasha. That's it.'

Eden frowned. 'What does that mean?'

'It means that if Sasha hadn't been in this accident you wouldn't have come back home. I wouldn't have been an insensitive clod and we wouldn't be having dinner together.'

'But all of that *did* happen and here we are. Sitting at a candle-lit table in an Italian restaurant, discussing the way you were just looking at me. I know you have your world nicely under control and would rather not have it upset, but sometimes when our worlds are turned on their heads we find out more about ourselves.'

'Is that what has happened to you? Working overseas, helping so many people—has it helped you to know yourself better?'

Eden thought on his words. 'In a way it has, and in other ways I think I've lost myself even more.' The mask was off. There was no flirting, no laughter in her words. She was trusting him with a much deeper side of herself. 'It's strange. Coming home like this… I didn't realise how much I'd…missed.' She played with her food for a moment before putting the fork down and pushing the plate away.

'Do you mean your family?'

Eden sighed and met David's eyes. There he was. In the role of confidant, the man she could trust, could talk to, could rely on to tell her what to do. 'I left Sydney with such anger, such determination to show my parents that I didn't need their money to have a wonderful life.'

'And on the whole has it been wonderful?'

She nodded. 'It hasn't been too bad. I supported myself through medical school, and I've worked in some incredible places, met some amazing people and travelled the globe. I love helping people.'

'I know.'

'It's very fulfilling—especially where there is poverty. Being able to make such a difference, to see that what you personally are doing is changing things for the better. It's a nice feeling.'

'I don't doubt that. You've been helping people for so long, Eden. Even when you were young you were helping those around you. But your family are a part of you. Your parents. Your brother. They're in your heart and won't ever leave, despite how long it's been since you've seen each other.'

'Is that how you feel about your parents?'

'My parents had an indifferent attitude to their children. Being raised by nannies and housekeepers wasn't all that bad. Sasha and I had every possible material possession we could need.'

'But not your parents' love?'

He nodded. 'As an adult it's easier to under-stand why our parents did what they did. They didn't know any different. They both came from wealthy families, were raised by nannies and sent to boarding school at young ages them-selves. They married because it was expected of them, and they produced offspring.'

'And all that because of money—because of wealth.' The sour taste which had made her flee her own house all those years ago rose in her mouth. 'At least your parents have the excuse of being raised in that environment. They didn't know any different. *My* parents did. They won the lottery when I was ten, moved to the upper north shore and changed our lives—for the worst.'

'That was a long time ago, Eden. Perhaps this feeling you have now of missing something is because you're ready to see them. Surely the possibility must have crossed your mind when you made the decision to come home?'

'Of course it did. But Sasha is my first respon-sibility. She needs me and I'm here for her.'

'For how long?'

'You asked me that earlier today. As long as it takes.'

'What if that's months?'

'Then I'll be here for months.'

David was a little surprised at this. 'I thought you'd just taken leave for a few weeks?'

Eden shook her head. 'No.'

His eyes widened. 'You've resigned?'

She smiled. 'I've taken an indefinite leave of absence. In other words, I've asked PMA not to send me anywhere just now.'

'That's Pacific Medical Aid, right?'

'Yes.'

'I have a friend who's done a lot of work with them over the years.'

Eden was surprised. 'Who?'

'Michael Hill. Do you know him?'

'Yes. Of course. I've worked with both Michael and his wife, Chloe, on several occasions in Tarparnii. They have two absolutely gorgeous children.'

'Two? I knew they had a little girl. She had one of those new-fangled strange names which seem to be so popular.'

'Meeree is her name—and it's not new-fangled. She was named after a very good friend of theirs. They've also adopted a little Tarparniian boy, Worf, who can climb trees faster than anyone else I've seen.' She shook her head. 'Wow! I can't believe you know them.'

'The world isn't really that large. When you narrow your parameters it becomes quite small, quite intimate, and that's why it's a good idea to see your parents while you're here.'

Eden listened to his words, watching his expression. The waiter came and cleared their plates, yet she kept her eyes on David. When they were alone again, she asked carefully, 'Why are you so insistent that I should see my parents? Is something wrong? They're both well, aren't they? David, you would tell me if something was wrong, wouldn't you?'

'They're both fine, Eden.'

'Which means you're in contact with them.'

'Yes. *I* wasn't the one who ran away from home.' He didn't think it the right time to let her know that her father, Hal, was also his tennis partner. David had always respected Eden's parents, and when he'd returned to Sydney he hadn't seen any reason not to continue the friendship.

'I didn't run away. I was told to leave. My father kicked me out—remember?'

'Actually, I don't. I was in Melbourne at the time.'

'You know, if you *had* been here in Sydney perhaps things wouldn't have escalated so badly between my father and myself.'

'Your rift is *my* fault now?'

'No. It's just that you were my sounding board. You were my voice of reason. I listened to you. I looked up to you—especially in your first year of medical school. Until then you were just Sasha's big brother—my surrogate big brother—there to help us out when we needed you. But that year, David, when I helped you study, when we would talk about anything and everything long into the night, when we became friends—real friends in our own right and not just because of Sasha—that was one of the best years I've ever had.' Tears touched her eyes for the second time that night. 'And then you left me.'

She dragged in a breath, trying to keep her emotions under control. 'I missed you so much, and not just because of our attraction. I missed our talks. I missed your voice of reason. Your clarity of mind. Your guidance. Your support.'

'So are you saying if I'd stayed you wouldn't

have organised a protest march—a *public* protest march—against your father's own company?'

'He was in the wrong. The health of his factory employees was at stake. I'd tried to reason with him. I'd given him fair warning of what I thought, of what I had planned in the way of protest, and still he didn't do anything about it. The protest was a success. His company was forced to take action. Nowadays there are occupational health and safety measures put in place by the government.'

'A win?'

'Politically, yes. Personally, no.' She sighed. 'I don't know if I'd have done anything different. I just know you would have helped me to perhaps look more closely at the possible repercussions—because I would never have guessed that my father would ask me to leave his house.'

'The past is the past and we can't change it. I can't change my parents and I don't even bother trying. I see them twice a year at their Easter and Christmas parties, and I send an appropriately expensive gift on their birthdays. That's it. I can't change them, Eden, but your parents are different. They've changed themselves. There have been a lot of hard lessons for them to learn—for you all to learn. Surely it's time to try and patch things up again?'

'Do they know I'm in Sydney?'

'They know about Sasha's accident. They're smart enough to figure out the rest. And as you're planning on staying for a while, the longer you leave it, the harder it will get.'

'The voice of reason?'

David's smile was small, but it radiated kindness. 'If you like.'

'I'll sleep on it.'

'Good—and speaking of sleep, how about I get you back to your hotel?'

'Nice segue, Dr Montgomery.'

'Thank you, Dr Caplan.'

As they left the restaurant, Eden realised the temperature had dropped. It still didn't compare to the wintry weather in the Ukraine, but it was cool enough to make her shiver. Without a word, David slipped off his jacket and placed it around her shoulders.

'Thank you.' They'd taken but a few steps when Eden tripped, but David quickly steadied her. 'Sorry. I told you I wasn't too good at walking in high heels.'

'I remember.' He had his arm about her waist

and decided it was probably easier to keep her warm and support her by leaving it there. Glad he'd found a logical reason to hold her close, to torture himself with her soft body against his, he started them on their way back to her hotel. When they stopped at a pedestrian crossing, Eden leaned against him, closing her eyes and breathing in deeply.

'Mmm. You smell like you,' she mumbled, and he realised she was getting sleepier by the minute…and more difficult to resist.

'We're almost there.' He put his other arm around her, holding her firmly as they waited for the light to change. He closed his eyes and tucked her head farther into his chest, breathing her in. Eden. Gorgeous, impetuous, delectable Eden. He'd been hard pressed the whole night long to stop himself from doing what he was doing now…holding her close.

He ignored the rational side of his mind—just this once—not wanting to be bothered about analysing exactly what this meant. Instead he allowed himself the luxury of simply enjoying her being this close, snuggled into him, resting sleepily against his chest. Even all those years ago he'd never held her like this, and although they were now surrounded by the sounds and colours of city life it didn't seem to matter.

The fact that she fitted perfectly into his arms, that her body moulded against his as though they'd been made for each other, *did* matter— and it was something he knew he'd get used to far too quickly. He'd been surprised and then touched when she'd told him how much she'd missed him the year after he'd left Sydney.

Feeling jostled from behind, David opened his eyes and belatedly realised that they'd missed their turn at the lights. Eden was now dozing against him, her exceedingly long day finally catching up with her. The need to protect this woman surged within him once more, and as he watched the traffic flow by he knew the feelings he was trying to deny wouldn't stay hidden for ever.

When the lights turned green, he managed to rouse her long enough to get her across the road, into her hotel and in the lift up to her room. 'Where's your key, Eden?'

She sighed as she leaned into him, and mumbled something which sounded like 'purse'. He took it from her hands and found the swipe card to open the door. He managed to prop the door open, but by that time she was barely able to stand on her feet. It appeared jet lag had finally hit, and he sympathised with her.

Lifting her into his arms, he carried her over the threshold and into the room, thankful that the maids had been round to turn down the bed. He slipped his jacket from her shoulders, then laid her down before removing her shoes and the clip from her hair. She snuggled instantly into the pillow and David folded the bedcovers over her.

He leaned forward and placed a kiss on her forehead. 'I missed you, too.' He brushed her hair from her face, his fingers grazing the softness of her skin. The touch electrified him and he quickly stepped back, looking at the sleeping woman, his heart pounding out a tattoo.

Never had he felt this way about any woman, and that was a scary thought. She was Sasha's best friend, she was Hal's daughter and she would soon become a temporary hospital employee. To become more involved with Eden would not only hurt her…it would hurt him as well.

CHAPTER FIVE

THE next morning Eden woke to the incessant ringing of the phone beside her. Reaching out, she grabbed the receiver and lifted it to her ear.

'Hello?' she mumbled, her eyes still closed, the remnants of an incredible dream involving David Montgomery swirling around in her mind.

'Wakey, wakey. Rise and shine,' a deep, rich voice said down the line. It sounded just like David, and she snuggled deeper beneath the covers, thinking she was still dreaming.

'Hmm. Instead of me rising, why don't you come over and I'll show you how we can both shine together.'

'*Eden!*'

He lowered his voice, and she chuckled at the veiled desire she could hear threaded through his tone. She'd always been able to razz David up. It had been one of her favourite things to do, and she was enjoying the way he now seemed to be accepting her teasing and wanting her to continue. Mmm, this was a very good dream. A little more intricate than the ones she usually had about him, but still, she wasn't going to quibble with her imagination.

Her laughter ended on a sigh. 'I've missed you, David. Why do you have to be so far away? Come and cuddle me. I know you've always wanted to cuddle me, to hold me close in a nice big bed.' She knew her bed in the PMA dorm wasn't what you would call big, but they could squeeze in.

'Eden…'

Her fuzzy mind started to wake a little, and she idly wondered when she'd had a phone installed beside her bed. There was the phone in the corridor outside her room. That was the one which usually rang at all hours. She frowned and opened one eye, taking in the unfamiliar surroundings. Where *was* she? Her mind frantically began to sift through the last memories she could recall as she moved in the bed, discovering that it was indeed big.

'Sasha!' She sat up suddenly, remembering where she was and why.

'Sasha's fine,' David said down the line. 'Are you all right?' There was concern in his tone and

Eden closed her eyes in embarrassment as she recalled exactly what she'd just said to him. Hopefully, though, he'd think she was just being her usual teasing self—yet in actual fact she'd been serious...seriously dreaming of him. Again.

'Yeah. Yeah, I'm fine. I'm OK. So...what time is it?' She turned to look at the digital display on the hotel clock. 'After ten! My goodness. I didn't realise it was as late as that. Poor Sasha. I said I'd have breakfast with her.'

David chuckled. 'Perhaps you could make it lunch instead? At any rate, if you're able to come in to the ward to sign a few papers, your VMO status can be finalised.'

'That was quick.'

'I need your expertise, Eden.'

'Oh?' She smiled, taking his words out of context. 'Do you, now?' Her tone was rich and saucy, and she heard him breathe heavily into the phone.

'And then, later on today, I thought I might take you to see your family.'

She pouted. 'You don't play fair.'

'Neither do you. How are you feeling? Still fuzzy from the jet lag?'

Eden thought for a moment, then looked down at what she was wearing. 'I'm still in my dress.' The words were said with total surprise.

'Do you remember much about last night?'

'Of course I do. Except for getting back to the hotel. That's all a bit blurry.'

'You were exhausted.'

'I take it you were the one to tuck me safely up in bed?'

'Well, it was a toss-up between myself and the night concierge, but he was a bit of a weakling and wasn't strong enough to carry you.'

'You *carried* me?'

'It was either that or let you sleep in a puddle on the floor.'

'I guess thanks are in order, then—both for not leaving me in a puddle and for tucking me safely into bed.' She leaned back against the pillows. 'Thank you, David.'

'You're welcome, Eden. Now, what time can I expect you in?'

'You're all business this morning.'

'Some of us have to work.' There was something in his tone which let her know that things might not be going the way he'd hoped.

'Dart?'

'No change. It's so odd. I'm going to order the MRI.'

'Can we get him put into a private room? If his symptoms are puzzling, then perhaps he should be isolated.'

'Yes. I was thinking along those lines, too. If possible, I'd like you there for the MRI.'

'Let me know what time and I'll be there… Well, after you tell me where the MRI unit is situated, that is.'

'Thank you, Eden.'

'OK. I'd better ring Sasha and apologise for sleeping through our breakfast date.'

'She's at Physio at the moment, but I told her that you were exhausted last night.'

Eden raised her eyebrows at this news. 'Sash knows we went out to dinner?'

'Yes. Anything wrong with two old friends enjoying a meal together?'

She smiled at his words. 'No. Nothing at all—so long as you don't think it was *only* two old friends enjoying a meal together. From what I remember, there was quite a bit of flirting going on, too.'

'You're the expert.'

'I am.'

'So…I'll see you soon?'

'Give me half an hour and I'll meet you on the ward.'

'Half an hour? To get ready and walk to the hospital?'

'I'm used to moving quickly,' she supplied.

'See you then.' David replaced the receiver and leaned back in his chair. She was definitely moving quickly—moving quickly into his mind, into his heart, into his life. From the instant he'd laid eyes on her he'd found it increasingly difficult not to think about her. After holding her so close last night, feeling the softness of her skin, the silkiness of her hair…it had been impossible not to dream about her.

It was just the way it had been all those years ago—the way he'd thought about her, looked forward to spending time with her even though she'd been helping him study. Never before or since had study been so…evocative. Having her quiz him on the bones of the body whilst her scent had surrounded him. The way her laughter would mesmerise him if he got the answer wrong. How she'd lie on the floor with her sexy legs resting on his bed; medical textbooks surrounding her auburn locks as exhaustion started to set in.

Back then he would dream about her every night, which hadn't helped with his concentration when it came to actually sitting the exam. Now, though, he and Eden were adults. They had no parental interference, they'd qualified, had their careers firmly on track. It should all seem so simple. But it wasn't. He'd had one failed marriage and there was no point in even pursuing another one given that the outcome would be the same.

Women wanted children. Eden would want children. He couldn't give them to her, which meant she was better off with someone else. The problem was he was having a difficult time following through on his own plan. How hard *was* it to keep his distance from her?

Apparently very hard, because right now he was watching the clock, waiting for the next half hour to pass as quickly as it possibly could. He was still stunned at how open she'd been with him last night, telling him about her darkest time overseas. What was gnawing at him now was that he'd had an equally dark point, which had changed *his* life, and there was no way he wanted her to know.

As it stood, Jacqueline was the only person

who knew what had happened to him—and that was only because she'd been there when the verdict of his sterility had been passed. His parents, Sasha, none of his closest friends had any idea of the accident he'd been involved in almost seven years ago.

He'd dealt with it. He didn't need to rehash old war wounds with Eden. Besides, despite what he was feeling for her, he knew deep down she wouldn't stay in Sydney. She was a lone reed, blowing where the wind took her, helping people who needed help. Right now that was Sasha, but he was sure that once Sasha was back to her old self Eden would leave again.

Was that why he'd been wanting her to make peace with her family? To give her stronger ties and keep her coming back to Sydney? David shook his head. Eden needed to heal the rift with her parents if for no other reason than to help take away some of the sadness he'd seen behind her eyes.

The protectiveness surged within him again, and he knew if he didn't stop just sitting around thinking about her, he'd get nothing accomplished before she arrived at the hospital. He looked at the clock and groaned. He'd wasted another ten minutes thinking about Eden. The woman was trouble…but it was a trouble he was drawn to.

'Hi, Francie,' Eden said as she walked towards the nurses' station. 'How are things this morning?'

'Frantic,' Francie replied. 'I have an eleven-year-old girl suffering from an eating disorder in Room 3, refusing to let me put a drip in.' Francie gathered supplies as she spoke. The phone was ringing, but someone else quickly answered it, and two sets of visitors had just come into the ward.

'Want a hand?'

Francie looked at her, a little protective, and Eden quickly continued, 'I have dealt with this sort of problem before. Unfortunately anorexia nervosa and bulimia are disorders the world over.'

'OK. If you can convince her to let me put the drip into her arm, then I'll be mighty grateful.'

'Room 3?' Eden pointed to the left.

Francie nodded. 'Rooms 2 and 3 have cameras in them. Sometimes it's necessary for the patients own wellbeing that we monitor them at all times.'

'I understand completely.' The two women headed into the room, where Eden was introduced to Chelsea. 'Hi. I'm Eden. I'm a paediatrician.'

'I haven't seen you before.' Chelsea's sunken eyes looked uninterestedly at Eden for a moment, before moving to gaze out of the window once more.

'I'm only a visiting doctor here. I usually work overseas.'

'Yeah?' The tone was still bland, but Eden managed to pick up something else. The smallest hint of interest. She guessed Chelsea wanted to know more, but she certainly wasn't going to ask. If she didn't interact with those people trying to help her, then it was easier to hear the voices in her mind—the voices which told her not to eat.

'I've been all over Europe, and to China, India and Argentina. I've worked in Ethiopia, Africa, and until recently I was in the Ukraine.'

'Yeah?' That same tone, but this time Chelsea was looking at Eden as she spoke. If she could keep it up, establish some sort of bond with Chelsea, then that would be the first hurdle over. She wanted to make it clear to Chelsea that she was only here temporarily, that she wasn't a permanent employee of the hospital or some specialist brought in to talk to her. Sometimes if patients knew you weren't going to be around for long they would more often than not open up and tell you things they wouldn't tell their local doctor.

Eden felt David's presence behind her. She had no idea whether he was in the room or just outside the door, but she knew instinctively he was there. A small, delightful shiver of awareness trickled throughout her body, and whilst she wanted nothing more than to turn around and drink him in, she pushed her impatience aside and focused on the girl before her.

'Travelling is great. I love it. So many places to see. So many things to do. So many adventures to have.' Eden smiled as she remembered her last trip to Egypt. 'Do you know where Cairo is?'

'Duh! Egypt.'

That one answer was enough to show Eden that this girl had a desire…and one desire was all it might take to get her back on the rails again. Most eleven-year-olds had no idea where Cairo was, but it appeared Miss Chelsea was quite a smart little cookie.

'Right—well, the last time I was there I was

in a market and there were lots of pushy men trying to sell me things. One wanted me to buy watches, another had scarves, some had food, but one very pushy salesman wanted me to buy a carpet—a rug.' Eden came around the bed and sat down on the edge. Chelsea shifted away from her. It didn't matter, though, because she was still looking at Eden. 'Now, you might not think anything was wrong with buying a carpet. He even tried to tell me that his carpets were of the flying variety.'

Chelsea scoffed at that idea. 'A flying carpet! Did they think you were dumb?'

Eden smiled. 'I must have looked it. Anyway, I was looking at one carpet that was hanging up, admiring the work and the pattern, when I thought I saw something move to my right. I looked over, but all I could see were other carpets, rolled up in a big, bulky way. I went back to my study of the carpet I was consider-ing buying. And just then...' Eden leaned forward, her voice dropping a notch or two '...I heard a noise.'

Chelsea's eyes widened with interest. 'What sort of noise?'

'It's hard to describe, but it was sort of like a

far-off sound of someone talking—sort of muffled talking. It was really strange. The carpet seller tried to cough to cover up the noise, and it was then I realised that I *had* heard something.'

'Otherwise he wouldn't have tried to cover it up.' Chelsea spoke with authority, but Eden was just pleased she had the girl's attention.

'Exactly. So I pointed to the rug which was rolled up on the ground, and I said, in my bravest voice, "I'd like to see this one, please." Well, the owner tried to talk me out of it, pointing to other rugs and different carpets hanging up, already unrolled, giving me excuses and telling me he couldn't unroll it because it was too heavy and would take too long. He wanted me to buy, and buy quickly. He was becoming quite insistent.'

'What did you do?'

'I kept pointing to the one which was rolled up. "I want to see this one," I kept saying, and he kept trying to put me off. He was all dressed in robes, but as he moved I saw the folds of material shift back and noticed there was a gun in a holster on his back.'

'What?' Chelsea was in shock. 'Oh, my gosh! What did you do?'

'I kept insisting I wanted to see the rolled-up

carpet, and in the end I actually leaned down and started to push the carpet so I could roll it out. He hadn't been joking when he'd said it was heavy, but I persisted—even though he was trying to stop me, to pull me off.'

'But he might have shot you!'

'I know, but by then, we'd caused such a scene that other tourists had stopped to see what was going on. At first I think they thought it was a theatrical performance.' Eden shook her head and Chelsea rolled her eyes.

'Dumb.'

Eden smiled. 'Anyway, I kept rolling the carpet out, and as I did I realised that the reason I'd seen the carpet move and the reason why I thought I'd heard muffled yelling was because there was a man rolled up in the rug!'

Chelsea was dumbstruck, blinking her eyes several times in disbelief. 'Well? What happened?'

'The man who was in the carpet jumped to his feet, gasping for air and shouting at the carpet-seller in their native language. Then the carpet man pulled out his own gun and pointed it at the carpet-seller.'

'What did you do?'

'I kept asking them both to stop, but I don't

speak Arabic all that fluently, and there are so many different dialects I wasn't quite sure what I was saying. For all I know I was asking how much it was to buy a camel!' She laughed at her own silliness.

'Well…what happened next?' It was a deep, masculine voice that asked the question, and Eden turned to see both Francie and David as mesmerised by her story as Chelsea.

'Oh…yes. Well, obviously no one got shot—especially not me, because I'm still here—but it turned out the man who had been rolled up was a spy.'

Chelsea was so excited at this information that she clapped her hands. 'A real spy? You've met a real spy!'

'I have. His name was Tony.'

'Tony?' Chelsea scoffed. 'That doesn't sound like a spy name. It should have been James or Ranulf or something exotic.'

'Perhaps it wasn't his real name. Either way, he used my phone to call some of his colleagues and they came and took the carpet-seller away. Tony took me out for a drink—non-alcoholic, of course—to say thank you for saving his life.'

'Was he good-looking?'

'Tony?' Eden thought for a moment before shrugging. 'He wasn't classically handsome, but he was a nice man.' She glanced to her right and saw David shifting uncomfortably. She worked hard at hiding her smile. Surely he wasn't jealous? But it wouldn't hurt if he was. After almost admitting that she'd been dreaming about him this morning, she'd come to the conclusion that she should pursue the attraction which existed between them to see where it led. That was if David would let her.

'You've met a *spy*.' Chelsea's words brought her attention back into the room. 'A *real* spy. I can't believe it.'

'Neither could I—but, as I said, travelling means you can have lots of adventures.'

Chelsea sighed and leaned back against her pillows. 'Have you had lots more?'

'Oh, I've had plenty—and I have the promise of still more to come.' She glanced at David again as she spoke. He would *definitely* be an adventure.

'Will you come and tell me some more later?'

Eden smiled warmly. 'I'd love to. I'll see if I can find some photographs as well.'

'Do you have one of Tony?'

Eden shook her head. 'No, I don't. But I do have his telephone number, and he told me that if I was ever in Egypt again, or in a tight spot, to give him a call.'

'He'll rescue you.' Chelsea clasped her hands together in the way that young girls did when they thought something was romantic.

'Let's hope I'm not in a position to need rescuing. Anyway…' Eden stood from the bed. 'Francie's going to put a drip in your arm now, and I want you try and keep it in until I come tomorrow. Think you can manage that?'

Chelsea's eyes lost their brilliance within an instant, but she reluctantly agreed.

'I'll tell you all about how I met a sheikh of Dubai.'

'Where's Dubai?'

'Why don't you try and find out before tomorrow? I'm sure Francie could find an atlas for you to look at.'

'Certainly,' Francie said as she set things up.

'Great. OK, Chelsea. I'll see you later.' Eden smiled at the child as she walked from the room, David close behind her.

'That was quite a story,' he murmured as they reached the nurses' station. 'Is it true?'

'Every word.'

David shook his head. 'Still getting into mischief.'

Eden smiled sweetly up at him and fluttered her eyelashes. 'You weren't there to stop me. My knight in shining armour.' She clutched her hands to her chest as Chelsea had done, and sighed theatrically.

'You do that well.'

She dropped the pretence. 'Thank you. Besides, I didn't go looking for mischief—as you call it. Tony probably would have suffocated if I hadn't happened along. He was wrapped really tight.'

'Was he really not that good-looking?' The words were out before he could stop them. That seemed to be happening to him a lot lately.

Eden glanced up at him, astonished he'd asked the question but pleased he had. It showed he was interested in her, and it was just what she needed right at that moment. 'I'm not that shallow, David. I look at the person on the inside rather than what's on the outside.'

'Of course.'

'But for the record…' She took a step closer and brushed her fingers through his hair, grazing the top of his ear. 'He was nowhere near as good-looking as you.'

David swallowed, feeling exposed and uncomfortable and yet delighted at her words. He took her hand in his own and lowered it. 'Not here.'

She waggled her eyebrows at him. 'Then where?'

'Eden. We need to work. To focus.'

'I *am* focused.' She edged closer to him, bringing her other hand up to touch his hair, but he caught it before she got there.

'On work.'

'Oh. On *work*. Well, of course I'll focus on work…if you'd be so kind as to stop holding my hands.' She chuckled as he let go of her wrists.

'Maybe I should have let you sleep? It would have been an easier day.'

'Maybe you should have kissed me goodnight last night, because then we'd both be having an easier day.' Her tone was deep, rich and seductive, low enough for only David to hear.

'How do you know I didn't?'

Eden's eyes widened at this, but she knew that David would never have taken advantage of her. He just wasn't that sort of man. He always did the right thing, and last night wouldn't have been the exception. It did, however, present the most perfect opportunity for her to turn the flirting up by a notch or two. 'You did? Darn. That means I missed it. Well, there's nothing for it but a do-over.'

'A *do-over*? Do I want to know what that is?'

Eden winked at him and swished her hips. 'Oh, honey.' She nodded slowly. 'You'll *want* to know, all right.'

David closed his eyes for a second, determined to find some semblance of control. 'Why don't you go see Sasha? Say hello, get your giggles out, and then come back when you're ready to work.'

'I'll do that—and then I promise to *really* work it.'

'Eden!'

She smiled warmly at him as she left the ward, then stopped and called over her shoulder. 'Have Dart moved into Room 2.'

'Why Room 2?'

'Just a hunch. Room 2—OK?'

He nodded and watched her walk away, her hips swishing in a way he was positive was designed to drive him crazy. It was working.

CHAPTER SIX

WHEN David knocked on her hotel door that night, he wasn't sure which version of Eden was going to be answering the door. Was it going to be Dr Eden—the dedicated paediatrician who also seemed to be a minor miracle-worker? Was it going to be nervous Eden—the one who really wanted to see her family, but wasn't quite sure? Or was it going to be flirty Eden—the one who could tie him up in knots with one simple smouldering look from those amazing green eyes of hers?

He hoped it was either of the first two, as he was sure if she opened the door dressed in nothing more than a hotel robe, her *come hither* eyes inviting him in, he wouldn't be held responsible for his actions.

After Eden had spent some time with Sasha, she'd returned to the paediatric ward ready to concentrate. He'd been most appreciative of it, and of her help. She saw things differently and seemed able to read people, knowing instinctively what sort of help they needed to ensure their recovery.

Young Chelsea was a prime example. When he'd walked into that room and seen Chelsea listening eagerly to the story Eden was telling, he'd been surprised at how different the child had looked. There had been no problems afterwards with Francie getting the drip in place, and when Eden had returned from visiting Sasha she'd had a large atlas beneath her arm.

'Borrowed from the hospital library,' she'd declared as she'd handed it to Francie. She'd assisted with Dart's transfer to Room 2, and when David had enquired of Eden what her hunch might be regarding the young boy, she'd merely put a finger over her lips and shaken her head.

'I never discuss my hunches,' she'd whispered.

'Why not?'

'Because things always go wrong if I do.'

Her answer hadn't made any sense to him, but he didn't care. If she could solve the riddle of why Dart's health was up and down like a yo-yo, then he'd leave her to her hunches.

She'd done an informal ward round with him, meeting the other patients on the ward, talking to mothers, cuddling some of the toddlers who'd held out their arms to her. It was as though she wore a perfume which made everyone she came into contact with relaxed and happy. It didn't matter whether children were having serious treatment or were just in for a broken bone. They seemed to flock to her and she absorbed all of it, giving back twice as much as she received.

David frowned as he looked at the closed door, wondering why she hadn't opened it yet. He knocked again, a little louder this time. Had she backed out? He'd been delighted when she'd said she'd visit her parents, even if she would only go if he went too. The last thing he needed was more time in Eden's company.

'Sorry.' The door was opened a moment later. 'I'm on the phone.' She indicated the mobile at her ear. 'Won't be long,' she said softly. 'Sorry, Jett. You were saying?'

David walked in, looking around the room he'd carried her into last night. Now that the lights were on, he could see two suitcases, still half-packed, and other clothes lying about the room, over chairs and the end of the bed. Eden climbed onto the bed and sat cross-legged in the middle, leaning back against the pillows.

'You'll need to figure out what she's allergic to first. This reaction isn't normal.' She paused. 'Yes, I understand you can't stop all treatments, but at least ease off on perhaps two and see if the rash clears. Is it an eczema type of rash or—?' She listened to her colleague, but watched as David seemed to prowl about the room.

'Have a seat,' she whispered. David shrugged, as though he wasn't sure where to sit. 'Just throw those clothes into the suitcase.' She watched him do as she suggested, smiling when he placed everything neatly and gently on top of her bags. It was so…David.

'What about zinc? If you stop two of her meds and put her on zinc?' She frowned. 'Of course there's zinc. It's one of the minerals we *can* get. At least requisition some, and you'll get it in about a week's time.' She listened again, still watching David as he leafed through the hotel's compendium. 'Oh, David might know. Just a second and I'll ask him.'

He looked up at her. 'Problem?'

'We have a patient—eight-year-old girl who's developed a rash.' Eden gave him the rundown on what medications the girl was taking and the other particulars he needed to know in order to help her out.

'What about a straight course of antibiotics?'

'Tried that. Worked for about two days and then the rash came back. Next?'

'Steroidial ointment?'

'Can't get it for another two weeks. Next?'

'Umm… Is she itching?'

'Yes.'

'I like your idea about zinc. Zinc is good for skin problems.'

'Anything else you can think of? Think natural medicines if at all possible. It's easier to get our hands on them than pharmaceutical products.'

'Do you think the rash is food related? Drug related?'

Eden checked with Jett. 'Possibility of both,' she returned.

'The problem might actually be with the gut rather than anything else. If it's food related, check what she's eaten, and if it's drug related, the acids in her stomach might either be reacting to it or might not be able to break it down properly.'

'Yes. Yes. Good idea.' Eden related this information to Jett, and within another minute or two she was off the phone. 'Thank you. I appreciate it, and so does Jett.'

'Is he a colleague in the Ukraine?'

'He is. He's the one who speaks the language most fluently, so we all tend to fight over him when we need things translated.' She smiled. 'I mean literally fight over him. One time Lauren and I had an arm each, and we were tugging poor Jett in two different directions whilst arguing over who needed him first and why.'

'Who won?'

'Tarvon. He's a doctor from Tarparnii. He's absolutely huge and he just put both hands on Jett's shoulders and practically lifted him off the floor. It shocked us all—especially poor Jett.'

Her grin was wide and bright, her eyes shining with the memory, and she looked stunning. For the first time since he'd seen her again she wasn't wearing a skirt or dress. Instead she wore a pair of denim jeans and a pale pink knit top. The colour should be all wrong to wear with hair so deep and rich, yet Eden carried it off to perfection.

When he just stood there, looking at her, Eden's smile started to change. 'David?'

'Hmm? Yes?'

'Are you all right?'

He shifted and realised she'd caught him staring. It wasn't the first time she'd caught him today, and he knew, as he found it difficult not to watch her every chance he got, it wouldn't be the last.

'Of course.'

'You know, if you keep looking at me as though you want to eat me up, I might just have to let you.'

'Now, Eden. Don't sta—'

'Start? Too late, David. This thing between us started over twelve years ago, and while we've both had our own experiences you have to admit it's quite astonishing to find the chemistry between us still alive and kicking.'

'It doesn't mean we need to act upon it.'

'We might if my heart-rate doesn't settle down. Whenever I'm around you it's as though it's beating out a samba.' She took a step towards him, closing the distance. 'You wouldn't want me to be having palpitations now, would you, Doctor?'

'Eden.'

'You're a caring doctor. One who has his patients' best interests at heart.' She continued to advance slowly, her steps small but sure, until she came to stand before him. He wanted to step back, to put more space between them, but he knew she'd follow him around the small hotel room.

'You're not my patient.' He looked down into her face, his voice deep and husky. If she'd had any doubts as to whether or not he wanted her to stop, they were dispelled in that instant. Hearing the repressed desire, seeing it in his eyes, noticing the way his hands were clenched into fists at his sides, as though he was trying desperately not to touch her, Eden knew he wanted to kiss her just as much as she wanted him to.

'Do I need to make the first move?' she whispered, her breath fanning over him, her alluring scent drawing him in. David placed his hands onto her shoulders, mainly to stop her from coming closer, to stop her from pressing her body against his—because if she did that, he knew he wouldn't be able to resist. Holding her close last night when she'd been asleep had been torture enough. It was ten times more acute now that she was awake.

'Eden. We can't.'

'Why not? You want to, David. I can see it in your eyes.'

'Of course I want to kiss you, to see what it's

like, to see if the magic is still there, but I can't.'
The grip of his hands on her shoulders intensified a little. 'I can't do that to you.'

'I don't understand. You admit you're attracted, and we both want it. We like each
other—we're friends. We've been dreaming
about this moment for a very long time, both
eager for the command performance. I think
we're ready.'

'I don't.'

'But you've just said that—'

David dropped his hands and stepped around
her, making sure their bodies didn't touch. He
walked towards the door, putting space between
them, his back to her.

'David?'

He closed his eyes, hearing her confusion. It
was just as it had been twelve years ago, when
he'd been forced to break her heart. She'd said
his name then, too. With the same tinge of hurt
and confusion lacing that one word as it did now.

'Talk to me. Tell me why we can't at least see
where this incredible thing between us might
lead?'

'Because I know where it will lead, Eden. I've
been down that road and it wasn't pretty.'

'What road? Your parents aren't involved in your life any more. They can't control what you do.'

'It's not my parents I'm talking about. I'm talking about serious relationships.' He turned then, looking at her, holding her gaze. 'You're too special to Sasha, too special to your family and too special to…' He stopped and swallowed before continuing, his tone a little more intense. 'You're too special to me.'

'For what? What are you talking about? It's good that I'm special to you. Isn't it?'

'Eden, I've had one failed marriage.'

'Marriage?' Her eyes widened at the word.

'I'm not a safe bet when it comes to serious relationships. We're both better off right now if we just ignore whatever exists between us and leave it at that.'

'David? You're not talking sense.'

'To kiss you would only draw us both in further. We know that. This thing between us is strong, stronger than anything I've ever felt before, and that in itself is reason enough why we shouldn't pursue it.' He laughed without humour and raked a hand through his hair. 'If my feelings for you are greater than they were for my ex-wife, then we're both in for a bucket-load of pain, and I don't want to hurt you.'

'I'm too special?'

'Exactly.'

'What happened in your marriage, David? Talk to me. Tell me. We're friends first and foremost. Surely you can trust me?'

'It's not a matter of trust, Eden.'

'I think it is. What went wrong? You know, it could have just been that you were married to the wrong person. You said yourself that you were sort of pressured into marriage by your parents, so it can't have been right in the first place. I'm different. I'm special, and you have stronger feelings for me. That's a good thing. Right?' She took a step towards him, but he equalled it by taking one back. 'And besides, your parents don't even likc me, so there's no way they'll ever pressure you to marry me.' She shook her head. 'Not that I'm suggesting we get married. Nor am I trying to pressure you into marriage—or anything else for that matter.'

'You're not? You're not trying to pressure me into kissing you?'

She shook her head sadly and sighed. 'No. I don't want to pressure you to do anything, David. I would, however, prefer it if you *wanted* to kiss me. Or even if you wanted to talk to me, to tell me what happened to break up your marriage—because from what you're saying I'm getting the feeling that it was much more than the reasons you've stated.'

He looked away and shook his head. 'I should have remembered I'm with a woman who can read other people like a book.'

'Hey—it's instinctive. It's like a gift. I didn't ask for it. I've had it most of my life.' She shrugged. 'I just understand people.' She smiled at him a little sadly. 'Most of the time.'

'Yet you're still trying to find out who *you* are.' His words were a statement of fact.

'And it appears you have the gift too.'

'No.' David shook his head. 'I just know you, Eden, and I see a lot of unhappiness behind your eyes.'

'Then why not help me with that by kissing me? That would definitely make me happy.'

He was thankful the tension in the room had returned to a more reasonable level, and he gave her a lopsided grin. 'This is you not pressuring me?'

'I'm not *pressuring*. I'm *cajoling*. They're two very different things.'

David stood there for a second before sliding his hands into the back pockets of his jeans. She hadn't missed the way he'd looked when he'd strolled into her room. Casual black jeans, white shirt and dark jacket. Simple, solid, and down-right sexy. Even now her fingers itched to touch him, to feel the firm contours of his chest beneath her splayed hands.

'Don't look at me like that.' His words were combined with a gravelly thread of want and desire, and it was then Eden realised she was giving him the once-over with her eyes.

'Sorry. I can't help it that I like looking at you.'

He clenched his jaw tightly. 'We need to go. Your family is waiting.'

Eden closed her eyes. 'Don't remind me.'

'If you don't want to go, if you're not ready yet, you can always cancel,' he suggested, trying to be helpful.

'No. I need to do this. It's like ripping off a sticking plaster. The sooner I do it, the sooner it's over and done with. It's the right thing to do, regardless of the unwelcome reception I'll no doubt receive. I need to do this for *my* sake, for *my* peace of mind.'

'You won't be unwelcome.' He could see

painful memories of the past wash over her, and his protective instinct reared its head again.

'How do you know? I mean, I'm presuming you've told them I'm coming round, right? There would be no point in going to see them if they weren't home.'

'They know you're coming and they *want* to see you, Eden. Your reception won't be a cold one,' he repeated.

'How do you know?' she asked again, even though she had an inkling of what the answer might be.

'I see your father quite a bit.'

'Is that so?'

David nodded. 'We play tennis together once a week.'

'Tennis? You play tennis?' The image came of him in white shorts and shirt, running around on a court, his muscles bunched and rippling. No wonder he was so toned.

'You're missing the point.'

'I hope you don't,' she joked, but he merely gave her a look which she knew of old meant that he wanted her to be serious. 'Sorry. Nervous humour.'

'They all miss you, Eden. Especially Todd.

They're all stuck in their daily grind and they need a little light in their lives. You can provide that.'

'But you will stay with me the whole time, won't you?'

'Yes.'

'Promise?'

'I promise.'

'Pinky swear?' She held out her little finger to him and David couldn't help but smile at the gesture. He'd seen her and Sasha do their 'pinky swear' promises for years. He slipped his little pinky around hers and squeezed, ignoring the way the simplest touch of his skin against hers made his heartbeat pound double-time.

'Pinky swear,' he repeated, before quickly letting go. 'So…ready?'

Eden nodded. 'As ready as I'll ever be.' She collected her purse, ensuring she had the hotel keycard inside, before David held the door open for her. They walked to his car in silence, Eden's thoughts fixed on the memory of the last time she'd spoken to her father.

Before she'd packed her bags and left, there had been some harsh words spoken, some unforgivable things said. They'd often argued way back then, mainly about the lifestyle her parents had been sucked into and how she had the right to disagree with them. Then she'd been asked to leave.

So she'd squared her shoulders and marched forward into her life—alone. She'd paid for herself to go to medical school, the hard way—without help from Mummy and Daddy. She'd paid off her student loans and was now debt free, doing what she did best—helping other people.

She remained silent on the drive, feeling the warmth of David's glance on her every now and then, pleased he wasn't trying to force her into talking. As he turned into Cherry Tree Lane, the street she'd live on for eight years, Eden felt a tightening in the pit of her stomach. He slowed the car down, coming to a complete stop as he parked at the kerb. She looked over at number 17—her parents' mansion—which was only partially visible due to the large brick wall and iron gates which ringed the property.

'Eden? Are you OK?'

'I think so.' She kept on looking at the house. Funny, she remembered it being bigger. 'It seems so strange being here.'

'You know, I've never asked, but did you get along with your parents before their big lottery win? Was it just their instant multi-millionaire status which annoyed you?'

'We got along fine before their win. Well, I was only ten. It was when we moved to this elite neighbourhood that things started going wrong. We didn't fight, per se, but I guess I baffled them more than anything. There they were, giving me everything I'd ever wanted, everything money could buy, and they couldn't understand why I wasn't happy, or why I'd give half of the presents away to others who had nothing. Sometimes, especially during my teenage years, they'd look at me with such puzzlement—as though to say, "Where *did* she come from?" Todd, however, was more their mould. A real chip off the old block, with a tiny bit of my zaniness thrown in.'

Eden sighed. 'I guess when I left, he saw that as total desertion.' She shrugged. 'But, to answer your question, for the most part even after the big win I thought I got along fine with my parents. *They* probably wouldn't agree, as I think I caused them plenty of headaches.'

'You caused me a few, too.'

She smiled at his words. 'All I know is I was glad it was you who came down to the local police station to bail Sasha and I out after we were arrested for protesting and not my dad. I doubt I ever would have heard the end of it.'

'You're just lucky they were all out of town at a charity event and I knew the guy behind the desk at the police station.' David shook his head, remembering. It had been a week before he'd left—a week before his father had decided to change their worlds. 'Why were you arrested again?'

'For chaining ourselves to the front of a heritage building they were going to knock down. And I'll have you know that building still stands. I saw it when I came into town.'

'Another one of Eden's victories?'

'Yes.'

'So it was all worth it then?'

'Absolutely. Although I think being put in a gaol cell was almost the final straw for poor Sasha. For years I'd been dragging her along with my crazy antics, but while we were sitting on the small bed in the cell she looked at me and said, quietly and calmly, "You're my best friend, Eden, but being in here does upset me a little."' Eden laughed at the memory. 'Poor Sasha. She wasn't in tears or hysterical or anything, but she was mildly upset about being in there in the first place. After that she only came along to my protests when she agreed with them, and never again were we locked in a gaol cell together.'

'Well, that's good news.' She had her hands clasped together in her lap and he could tell by the way she was talking non-stop that she was nervous. 'It's time,' he said softly. He'd given her a few minutes in the car, not wanting to rush her, but he knew if she had her way they might sit in the car all night long.

'Yes.' She nodded, but didn't move.

David climbed from the car and came around to open her door. Still she didn't move.

'Eden?'

'Hmm? Oh, right. Time to go in.' She unclasped her seat belt and stepped from the car as childhood memories began to return. She looked up and down the street, noticing the size of the trees and how much the bricks in the wall had aged. 'Don't you think it's odd that Cherry Tree Lane doesn't actually have any cherry trees in it?'

'I do,' he replied as he shut the door after her and locked the car.

'Who thinks up these street names?'

'Someone who thought it sounded pretty.'

'I suppose so.' She stood on the footpath, noticing the old-fashioned street lamps shining bright beneath the starry sky which was starting to darken. Eden closed her eyes for a moment, breathing in deeply, the scents of her childhood returning.

'All right, all right—enough stalling.' David took her hand in his, giving it a small tug. 'You've looked, you've smelt. Time to move.'

She opened her eyes and grimaced at him. 'No fooling you, is there?'

'No, and you'll do well to remember that. Now, come on.'

Her legs felt like lead as she walked stiffly beside him. 'Remember you promised to stay with me?'

'I will.'

'You won't leave me alone with anyone?'

'Not unless it's what you want.' They were almost at the gate, where she knew David would press the intercom button and announce their arrival.

'What if they don't let me in? Don't tell them I'm here. Just say it's you,' she said quickly.

'They know you're coming, Eden.'

'Fine.'

'Can we please just make it to the other side of the gate?' David pressed the button and announced his name. A moment later an electronic buzz sounded and the gate opened.

'And make sure you take me back to my hotel. I don't want to stay here. I won't be pressured.'

'I promise to take you back to the hotel.'

They were walking up the path which would lead directly to the front door. How many times had she climbed over the brick wall and ran helter-skelter across the grass, sometimes dodging the sprinklers, other times strolling through them, especially on hot days? 'Wow, the ground looks really dry.'

'Water restrictions.'

'I know, but I didn't expect it to be this bad for some reason.'

'We've had quite a few dry summers.'

They were almost at the door, and Eden's grip tightened on David's hand. She pulled him to a stop at the bottom of the steps. 'It will be all right, won't it?'

He took both her hands in his and gave them a little squeeze. 'It'll be fine. You'll be fine. It's time.'

'Yes. It's time.' She could hear footsteps approaching the front door, and David held her gaze.

'Best behaviour, now. No picking fights. This is a time for reconciliation.'

Eden didn't say anything, but watched as the front door opened and she came face to face with her father.

They stood there, staring at each other for a brief moment, before her father shocked her completely by throwing his arms about her and embracing her so fiercely she thought she might pass out.

'Eden? Is it really you?'

She clung even tighter to David's hand, giving it pulsing squeezes.

'You might want to loosen up there, Hal. She still needs oxygen,' he drawled.

'Oh, right. Sure. Come in. Come in.' He stepped back, allowing them to enter the wide entrance hall. 'David's here,' he announced to the house in general. 'And he's brought a special friend. We didn't tell Todd,' he said more quietly.

'Why not?'

Hal shrugged. 'He may not have been here if we had.'

Eden had expected the pain, she'd known it would come, but she hadn't expected it to hurt this much. 'I see.'

'I'm sorry, Eden. That came out rather

abruptly. Todd's a busy man now. He has his own life.' Hal tried to justify things as best he could.

'It's OK, Dad.'

'It's good to hear you call me that.' Her father smiled and reached out to take her hand. It was then he realised that one of them was still being firmly held by David. He glanced quickly at one and then the other, before clearing his throat and leading them into the living room. 'Come in. Please come in. Todd?' he bellowed.

'I'm coming.' The sound of her brother's voice made Eden tense all over again. True, her father's reaction wasn't what she'd expected—far from it—but how would her brother react?

'Hey, David. Did you see the final score? Straight sets,' Todd commented on his way into the room. When he saw Eden, he merely glanced at her before returning his attention to David, his face expressionless. 'So? Who's your friend?'

'Todd…' Hal growled.

The pain of rejection pierced her heart. 'It's all right, Dad. Todd's entitled to his feelings.' He'd certainly grown up. Her brother was indeed a man, and she'd missed it—missed his journey. She couldn't blame him if he hated her.

'No. This is a time for celebration. Time to kill the fatted calf.' He put his arm around Eden and hugged her once more. Still she didn't let go of David's hand. It was as though they were fused together. He was her lifeline and she needed him. 'I have my family together again.' He let her go and smiled warmly, dropping a brief kiss on her head. 'Where is your mother?'

'I'll get her,' Todd offered, and quickly left the room.

Eden glanced at David, who nodded encouragingly.

'Sit down, sit down,' Hal invited. 'Your hair is as gorgeous as ever, Eden. Your grandmother had hair that colour. That's where you inherited your fiery spirit from.'

'Really?' She hadn't ever heard that before.

'Oh, yes. She caused havoc back in her day. Well, until your grandfather tamed her.' Hal chuckled. 'Having a family settled her down. You'll be the same.'

Eden blinked. 'Pardon?'

'Drinks,' Hal continued. 'You both need a drink. What will it be?'

'Iced water would be great,' David said.

'Eden?'

'Er…fine…water's fine.'

'Great. Be right back.'

To Eden's astonishment, her father left the room to go and get them drinks. Where were the servants? The butler opening the door? The maid getting their drinks? Within twelve months of them arriving at this enormous house her father had insisted her mother needed help, and help they'd received. The 'help' had increased slowly over the years, until her father had employed a household staff of ten to potter around after them, waiting on them hand and foot. It had been too much for Eden to bear back then, but now there didn't seem to be a member of staff anywhere. Perhaps it was late? Maybe they'd gone home?

'I don't understand,' she whispered. 'Where are all the servants?'

'We don't have permanent staff any more,' her mother's cool, modulated voice came from the doorway and Eden immediately looked her way. Gretchen Caplan was sophistication at its best. If anyone had been born to have money, it was her mother. She was a woman who'd always carried herself with flair and poise, and now, dressed in casual pants and shirt, was no exception. 'We have a house-cleaner, of course, but that's only once a week.'

Eden stood, and so did David. 'Hello, Mum.'

'Eden.' Her mother nodded. 'Please sit. Be comfortable. David, lovely to see you as always.'

'You too, Gretchen.'

Todd re-entered the room, and a moment later Hal returned with the drinks, handing them out with forced joviality. Eden felt uncomfortable, as she was sure did everyone else. She took a sip of the water and forced a smile, one hand still clinging tightly to David. She was sure she was cutting off his circulation, but he wasn't saying anything so she pushed that thought from her mind.

'So,' her father drawled into the tense silence, 'tell us what you've been doing. Working hard?'

'Yes. I've been…ah…overseas. Working in small villages and orphanages.' She shrugged. 'Being a doctor.' She wasn't sure what else to say.

'You're back for Sasha, I take it?' her mother said.

'Yes.'

'It doesn't matter about the reason,' Hal added. 'She's here.'

'It took Sasha to be almost at death's door to make you come home? What? Couldn't be bothered making it back for her wedding?' Todd sneered.

'That's enough.' David's tone was quiet, yet firm. 'All four of you are starting to drive me mad. Regardless of the reason why Eden is back in Sydney, the point is she's back. She has her own life and she's not accountable to any of you, just as you are not accountable to her. Now, you're either going to let the past be the past or let it interfere with your future for the *next* ten years.' He shook his head. 'Honestly, when they were handing out stubbornness this family certainly received its fair share.'

'Hear, hear!' Hal agreed, his tone now more sincere, more relaxed than before. 'Forgive and forget—and I certainly hope you can forgive me, Eden. I said some horrible things to you the night you left, and it's plagued me ever since.' He leaned forward and took her free hand in his, his voice shaky with emotion. 'Whatever reason it is that's brought you home, I'm just glad you're here, girl, and that I finally have the chance to say I'm sorry.'

A lump formed in Eden's throat and tears

welled in her eyes. 'Dad…' For the first time since she'd entered the house, she let go of David's hand so she could properly embrace her father. 'I'm sorry, too. Sorry for what I said.' She turned to her mother. 'Sorry for making you worry.' She looked at Todd. 'And sorry for deserting you.'

Todd stood there, hands shoved in his pockets, before shaking his head and stalking from the room. Eden quickly looked around at David, who merely shrugged.

'He'll come round,' Gretchen offered as she too embraced her daughter—but not with the exuberance of her husband. 'I'm relieved you're safe, Eden.'

They stayed another ten minutes before the headache pounding against her skull couldn't be ignored any longer. After promising to see them soon, Eden and David said their goodbyes.

It wasn't until they were seated in his car, heading back to her hotel, that Eden started to cry. She knew she needed to release the pressure building inside her, to let the emotions out. She'd never been good at bottling things up.

David didn't say a word, but just quietly passed her his handkerchief. By the time they

arrived at her hotel she was only sniffing inter-
mittently.

Again he came round and helped her from the
car, linking his hand with hers as they headed
inside. The silence continued as they walked to
the lifts, rode up to her floor. When they stood
outside her door, Eden jerked her thumb over her
shoulder, indicating the room behind them.

'Do you want to come in? I could make us a
cup of tea.'

David shook his head. 'I think it's better if I
go.'

'Are you sure? You were fantastic. Thank you
so much for being there, for supporting me. I
couldn't have done it without you.'

David shook his head. 'I don't know about
that. I'm really proud of you, Eden—and I don't
mean that to sound condescending or anything
like that. Going to see your family, breaking the
ice—it was a big deal. And for the record, I think
you would have managed just fine even if I
hadn't been there.'

'I disagree.' She put her hands on his shoulders and looked intently into his eyes. This
man, this man who was so special to her on so
many levels, this man who had held her hand

had given her strength. It wasn't the first time David had done that for her and she instinctively knew it wouldn't be the last. 'You were a good friend tonight, David. To all of us, but especially to me.' Standing on tiptoe, she kissed his cheek. 'Thanks.'

His hands came to rest at her waist. It was an automatic reaction to stop her from overbalancing when she leaned up to kiss him. He didn't remove his hands. Neither did she. David looked down into her upturned face, his gaze settling on her full and waiting lips.

Was he going to do it? Was he going to kiss her? Eden's breathing grew faster. Butterflies took flight in her stomach as she stayed completely still. She needed David to make this decision, to make this move. He'd been so adamant before that it wouldn't work between them, despite how much he wanted to kiss her.

Would he give in? Would he listen to his heart or his head? He glanced at her eyes, seeing total acceptance there. She was his. For this moment in time she was all his, and it was a moment he'd been longing for far too long to ignore any more.

'Eden.' Her name was barely audible on his parted lips, and she saw the raw heat, the full strength of his desire in his eyes as his arms tightened at her waist, drawing her closer.

This was it. It was finally going to happen. David was going to kiss her.

CHAPTER SEVEN

IT WAS as though he'd travelled back in time, to the first time his lips had pressed against hers, only this time he was not going to pull away. He was going to stay and he was going to enjoy it.

He lowered his head, coming closer to hers, drawing in her essence with every pounding heartbeat. He wanted to commit the minutest detail to memory, because he knew what they were about to do was wrong. Even though he knew the kiss would be earth shattering, it would no doubt be the last and final time he could hold her like this, could touch her like this, and he'd need something to keep him warm on the long, lonely nights which would stretch before him when she was gone.

The memories of her kisses, of the happier times they'd spent together, had helped him through the terrible sickness he'd suffered nearly seven years ago. *Eden.* The way she'd smiled. The way she'd felt in his arms. His mouth against hers. And now he was going to kiss her again.

When he was close enough, their lips parted, their breaths mingling… David closed his eyes, needing to concentrate completely on just what her mouth would feel like this time. Would it be different from all those years ago? Would the pleasure be as great now they'd both had so many life experiences? Would it be even better?

There was no time like the present to discover the answers. He touched his lips to hers.

The softness of her mouth captivated and enticed him, her scent winding itself around him, drugging him with its sweetness. This was real, this was now, and he wanted time to stand still so they could live in it for ever. It was as though she had been made for him, and deep down his heart begged him to acknowledge that truth.

Slowly, ever so slowly, he savoured the flavours of her, delighting in each one. The tart, the sweet, the seductive. She was everything he'd ever dreamed of, and he wanted to take his time exploring the lusciousness of Eden. His body taut with repressed desire, he gently slipped the tip of his tongue between her lips, knowing she would open to him—and she did.

She sighed into the kiss, loving the feel of his mouth on hers, and glad she finally had another memory to add to the ones which had managed to get her through some of the worst times in her life. Always when things were bad she would think of David and the happy times they'd spent together. Now…now she had more. She'd never been a greedy person, but she wanted him to kiss her again and again and again…for ever. She doubted she'd ever be able to get enough of the way he made her feel, the way her insides seemed to liquefy, her knees turning to a boneless mass at the slightest of touches from him.

He'd started the kiss in a slow and sensual way, and she'd been happy to go with that, but the raging torrent building inside her was threatening to rush forth and overflow if he kept up this pace. He was torturing her by so slowly and tenderly kissing her mouth, the tip of his tongue occasionally slipping between her lips, raising the overwhelming awareness which existed between them.

Inch by inch she brought her hands up his

chest, her fingers splayed as she tried to memorise every contour of his amazing physique. He moaned at the contact and she captured the sound into her mouth, taking the opportunity to gently nibble on his lower lip.

Stretching her arms up and winding them about his neck, she inched forward, her body now pressed hard against his chest. This time his groan was deeper, and as though something had snapped he plunged his tongue into her mouth. She reciprocated, opening up to him, needing him as much as he needed her.

At the ripe old age of nineteen he'd thought himself capable of resisting Eden, and when she'd kissed him, although the contact had been brief, he'd fought the attraction, knowing nothing could come of it. Now, at the age of thirty-one, he'd presumed himself more than able to kiss her and still hold onto some semblance of control.

He'd been wrong.

Where on earth had he got the idea that he'd be able to remain in control of his senses when she responded to him so ardently, so completely, so perfectly?

She was like a drug, and he knew after only

kissing her for a few seconds that he was definitely addicted. He'd wanted to know what it would be like to kiss her as the woman she'd grown into, not the teenager. Now he knew. And all he wanted to do was keep on kissing her again and again and again. For ever.

The hunger continued to rage between them, but there was also the need for oxygen, and in another moment he wrenched his mouth from hers, pressing small kisses to the corner of her delicious lips as he sucked air into his lungs. She did the same, and when she started to press kisses along his jawline and around his neck so she could nibble on his earlobe a shiver ran through him. He heard her deep chuckle in response.

'We are perfect for each other,' she murmured.

'You said that years ago, too.' David shook his head. 'Can you now see why I had to leave Sydney?' he muttered as he buried his face in her neck, breathing in deeply. 'You were so young. *We* were so young. I knew it was getting serious between us. Too serious.' His deep, whispered words washed over her as she continued to spread little kisses over his skin.

Eden eased back a little to look at him, her

eyes now a dark green filled with desire. 'So you gave in to your father because of me?'

'Yes. At first I wasn't at all happy with the idea of leaving. I wanted to be with you, and although I know I hurt you, in a way I meant what I said to you that night in the garden. We *were* young, Eden. Both of us. Filled with teenage ideals.' David looked down at her, unable to let her go just yet. The way she felt in his arms was right. He had no idea why, it just was. She was Eden. *His* Eden.

'You don't think it would have worked between the two of us back then?'

'We would have both gone to medical school. No doubt ostracised by our families and left without a penny to our names. It would have been difficult, and you might have grown to hate—'

Eden put a finger over his lips, effectively silencing him. 'Shh. It was just a question, and we *were* young. Because you left, our lives have gone in completely different directions. We've had a lot of different experiences which we might not have had otherwise.'

'Yet here we are.' He rubbed his fingers gently up and down her back and Eden snuggled deeper against him. He wanted to kiss her again, to devour her luscious mouth, bring her body as close to his as he possibly could. He needed her…*really* needed her…and until that split second he hadn't realised just how powerful that need was.

What had he done by kissing her? By ignoring the voice of reason? By giving in to his desires? He would hurt them both far more than he had in the past. She would be in town for a while. He couldn't quit his job in order to put distance between them. He'd have to see her at the hospital, at Sasha's house, but hopefully they'd be able to remain civil towards each other…at least until she returned overseas to her next PMA assignment.

'I like being in your arms,' she murmured against his chest. 'I like breathing you in.'

'I like holding you in my arms, your perfume winding around me.' He kissed the top of her head.

'Can it last?'

The question was quiet, but he felt the words against his chest, his heart constricting. David swallowed, unsure what to say, what to do.

Eden eased back and looked up at him. 'David? What do we do now?'

'I don't know, Eden.' He closed his eyes, wondering how he was ever going to tell her that he couldn't have children. When he and his ex-wife had realised the truth of that it had been the straw which had broken the camel's back. Would Eden understand where Jacqueline hadn't? Was he willing to take that risk by laying himself open to her? Jacqueline had hurt him badly with her reaction. Would Eden react the same way?

Eden sighed, loving the feel of him, the way his scent wound itself around her, becoming part of her. He was stroking her hair now, and she loved that too. She closed her eyes, knowing that after such an amazing kiss they had to figure out whether the attraction between them was worth pursuing.

It would mean drastic changes for her, and although she had an underlying feeling of discontent she still loved her job, and wasn't sure she could leave the employ of Pacific Medical Aid just yet. Would David wait for her? Join her for a brief stint in the field?

She opened her eyes. 'You said earlier tonight that it wouldn't work out between us.'

'I know.'

'You were adamant about it.'

'I know.' He looked down at her, down at that delicious mouth, and even though his mind was in turmoil his body knew exactly what it wanted. He pressed his mouth to hers, needing to live in the fantasy for a bit longer.

'Why not? Is it because of the directions we've gone in our careers? Is it impossible for us to make room for each other in our lives?' She leaned up and kissed him, savouring the taste and power. 'I've wanted to kiss you for so long. Now that we've given in to that I want more. I want to kiss you again and again. I want to hold your hand. I want to…dance with you in the moonlight. I want to wake up in the morning, to open my eyes and for you to be the first person I see.'

Eden threaded her fingers through his hair, gazing up into his beautiful eyes. One hand still stayed spread out across his heart, as though she couldn't bear to move it for fear that he'd let her go completely. Could she hold onto his heart just as he had a firm hold on hers?

'I dream about you. All the time. Even when I'm working overseas. I think about you all the time. About the fun we used to have. Even this morning I was dreaming about you.' Her cheeks coloured a little at the confession. 'When you called I thought I was still dreaming.'

'Ah.' David thought back to some of the things she'd said. 'I thought you were just trying to razz me up again.'

She smiled briefly, but her eyes were intent. 'You've affected me, David. For so long, in so many ways—and all of them are good.' She caressed his cheek, loving the way his five o'clock shadow felt against her smooth fingertips. 'Why do you think it wouldn't work between us?'

'Eden.' There was pain behind his eyes, and when he swallowed she reached up and placed a kiss on his neck, working her way up towards his mouth. He accepted her with the utmost pleasure, wanting to stay here, to live in this bubble where things couldn't go wrong, where they could figure out how to have the happy ending both of them wanted so badly. He wanted to lose himself in her, not to look forward, not to look back—just to…*be*.

This time when they kissed it wasn't like the other slow and exploratory episodes. This was hot, hungry and filled with the passion they felt for each other. His mouth was on hers with such pressure, such desire, such hedonistic pleasure.

'David,' she panted against his mouth when

they finally drew apart. 'I'm positive I'm in love with you. I know that probably makes things even worse, but—'

'It does. It means it doesn't matter what I do now—I'm going to hurt you.' He kissed her. 'I don't want to hurt you.'

'Talk to me,' she pleaded. 'Tell me what's going on in that intelligent mind of yours.'

He'd have to. He'd have to tell her about the accident, about the radiation sickness and about its inevitable outcome. She would be shocked, appalled, and she would leave him.

Holding her close, one hand on her head where she listened to the pounding of his heart—a heart that reciprocated the love she was offering—David knew it was time. Time to hurt them both. He couldn't do it here, though. Standing in a hotel corridor was not the right place.

'Tomorrow night?'

'We're having dinner with Sasha and Robert tomorrow night. I've already spoken to the nursing staff about getting her released for a few hours.'

'Good. She needs it. Hang on…*we're* having dinner?'

Eden lifted her head and smiled at him. 'You're supposed to come, too. I just kept forgetting to ask you.' She shrugged. 'A lot has happened since I got back to town.'

'You can say that again. So we're having dinner out tomorrow night? What about the day after?'

'So long as my temporary boss at the hospital doesn't take up my time with too much work, I should be available.'

He smiled, knowing she was trying to lighten the atmosphere. 'I'll take that into account.'

'Much appreciated, boss.' She kissed him.

David accepted the tantalising brush of her delicious mouth across his. 'You're addictive,' he murmured, and she laughed, the sound filling him with happiness. It had been so long since he'd had such happiness in his life, and now that it was back he didn't want to lose it again.

'Right back at ya, babe.' Her smile was too delicious for words, and he found himself lowering his head again.

'I don't seem to be able to stop kissing you,' he murmured against her mouth.

'Then don't.'

'Well, unless we plan to live in the corridor of this hotel, I think it's something we need to address.' As he spoke, he reluctantly eased his hold on her, releasing her from his arms.

'That doesn't mean you need to stop kissing me.' She pointed at the carpet, the place where they both stood. 'This isn't the only kissing Eden spot in all of Sydney, you know.'

'Eden, I—'

She placed a finger across his lips. 'Shh. Enough for tonight.'

David kissed the digit before taking both of her hands in his. 'OK. Go inside, get some sleep.'

'Sleep?' she repeated as he let go of her hands. Feeling bereft of his touch, she quickly dug around in her bag for the plastic keycard to the room. She found it and tried it in the door. It didn't work. 'These things hate me,' she muttered.

David merely smiled and took it from her, swiping it cleanly through. The door clicked open on the first go.

'Unfair,' Eden protested. She stood in the open doorway and turned to look at him, her gaze flicking from his lips to his eyes and back again. 'One for the road?'

'Hmm.' He slowly shook his head but grinned. 'You're incorrigible.'

'Only with you.' Eden sighed, pleased she affected him as much as he affected her.

With her smooth and delicious mouth against

his, David could feel himself capitulating once more, succumbing to her charms. He abruptly pulled away, his hands by his sides, knowing if he touched her it would take a lot longer for him to take his leave.

'Drive carefully,' she said softly.

'Sweet dreams.'

'I'll dream of you,' she promised, and laughed softly when he groaned.

'You're a tease, Eden Caplan.'

'But you love it. Goodnight, David.'

With that, he stepped back and allowed her to shut the door. He stood there for a few seconds, unable to move, unwilling to move. He placed a hand on the solid wood of the door, knowing she was just on the other side. So close, yet so far.

Eden leaned against the door, putting her hand up to the wood, knowing he was just on the other side. She closed her eyes and prayed, promising God she'd be a very good girl for the rest of her life if only she and David could work things out so they could be together. They just *had* to—because she was one hundred percent, prime-time in love with him.

* * *

When Eden arrived at the hospital the next morning—on time—she headed straight to the paediatric ward. She knew after talking to Sasha earlier that her friend had a physio session, but was really looking forward to escaping the bonds of the hospital that evening.

'I am too excited for words. It's the best thing. The absolute best. I've promised Robert I'll try extra hard in physio, and during my hydrotherapy session and everything, because today is going to be a good day,' Sasha had said.

'Sounds like an exhausting one, too. He's still not too keen for you to leave tonight?'

'He's worried. Wants to wrap me up in cotton wool.'

'I don't blame him. He loves you so much. But going out tonight will be good for him as well.'

'And, as I'll be escorted by two doctors, my own surgeon is not only fine with the arrangement, he's jealous he can't come with us.'

'Invite him along by all means. The more the merrier.'

'He's on call,' Sasha had added, giggling in a way which had brought an instant smile to Eden's face. Even now, as she walked onto the ward, she was smiling as she remembered how happy Sasha had sounded.

'You're looking bright and cheerful this morning,' Francie greeted her.

David was sitting beside Francie, frowning at some scans he was holding up to the light. He glanced over at Eden, but didn't say a word, his attention returning to the scans.

'I have a lot to be bright and cheerful about,' Eden said as she came around the desk, a small envelope in her hands. She placed it on the desk and picked up another scan which was loose on top of a radiograph packet. 'Dart's MRI?' she asked.

'Yes.' The child had required sedation yesterday while they'd been performing the scans, because any movement whilst the machine whirled around him wouldn't have been good.

'Anything?'

'What are these?' Francie interjected as she picked up the envelope Eden had put down.

'Pictures for Chelsea.' Eden frowned at the scans in much the same way David was.

'Ooh. May I have a look?' Francie was definitely eager.

'Sure.' Eden's attention was fixed on the

scans before her. 'David, there's nothing out of place.'

'I know.' He swapped scans with her and both of them continued to look. 'What are we missing? There's got to be something.' He threw the scan on the desk and raked both hands through his hair. 'It's so frustrating. Honestly, Eden. The other day he was running around like a little scamp, bouncing on his bed, telling me he didn't want the "yucky meddy", and in the next instant he was right back down again. Yet according to the scans and blood tests there's nothing wrong.'

'You've tested urine and faecal samples?'

'Yes. Apart from an increase in sodium he's fine, and the drip could account for that.'

'No improvement with the increase in fluids?'

'Mild. Not as much as I'd hoped.'

'You've seen him this morning?'

'Yes. No change. Still lethargic. Still not talking. His mother has suggested getting the surgeons in to perhaps do an exploratory.'

Eden concentrated on packing up the scans. 'He's still in Room 2, right?'

'Yes.'

Eden turned to Francie, who was oohing and

ahhing over some of the photographs she'd brought in to show Chelsea. 'Francie, you mentioned that Rooms 2 and 3 have video cameras in them?'

'Yes.'

'How do you view the footage?'

'The camera wasn't turned on in Room 2 last night,' David remarked.

'Um…actually, it was.' Francie shrugged apologetically. 'When I got in this morning the night sister told me that one of the enrolled nurses had turned on the camera in Room 2 rather than Room 3—which should have been monitoring Chelsea—by accident.'

'Chelsea wasn't monitored throughout the night?' Eden was a little concerned.

'No. Well, not via the cameras at any rate. She had her usual half-hourly obs and everything was fine with them.'

Eden picked up Chelsea's notes and read them. 'Good. This is good.'

'She's kept the drip in, the bags have been changed over at proper intervals, and there were no signs of self-inflicted drip removal.'

'Good. Well, in that case, if we have footage from Room 2, I'd like to see it.'

'I'll access it for you. Should take me about fifteen minutes to get organised.' A buzzer sounded and Francie rolled her eyes. 'Make that twenty.'

'Right. I'll go see Chelsea.' Eden picked up the photographs.

Francie started walking away from the desk, but stopped and came back, pointing to one of the pictures.

'And who is *that* gorgeous man?' she asked, indicating the photo of Eden and a man outside an elaborate Ukrainian Orthodox church.

'Hmm?' Eden looked at the photograph, conscious of the fact that David was peering over her shoulder. The heat from his body was warming her through and through, and she found it hard to resist leaning back a little so they were touching. To her surprise David shifted so that he could take her weight, not seeming at all concerned that they were so close in front of the nursing staff.

Eden tried to focus on what Francie had asked her. 'Ahh...the man? Er...that's Jett.' She sighed, letting David's spicy scent wash over her. 'That church is about two blocks away from where we live and work in the orphanage.' She sighed as she looked at the picture. 'It's such a beautiful building.'

'Stuff the building. I want the man. Is he single?'

Eden smiled. 'Yes. He's single.'

'Excellent.' Francie walked off.

'So that's Jett?' David's words brushed over her neck and down her spine before they burst into a flame of tingles which flooded her body. 'That's the man who called you last night?'

'Yes.'

'You look…friendly.'

Eden tried not to smile. 'That's because we're friends.' She turned her head to look up at him, knowing if she angled her shoulder just a touch she'd almost be in his arms again. 'Platonic friends, David.' He harumphed, and her smile increased. 'You're not…jealous, are you?'

'Huh.' He placed a hand at her waist, urging her forward. 'Let's go see Chelsea. I want to hear these stories, too.'

'What sort of answer is "huh"?'

'The only sort of answer you're going to get. Now, move it, Dr Caplan.' The warmth of his touch against her skin was starting to spread through her, and she knew if she didn't take his suggestion and move she would soon be incapable of moving at all—given that her limbs would have turned to mush.

'Yes, Dr Montgomery. Anything you say, Dr Montgomery. Your wish is my command, Dr Montgomery,' she flirted, batting her eyelashes at him.

'Eden.' There was a warning tone in his voice, but she could feel through the way his thumb was rubbing small circles against her back that he was enjoying the flirting as much as she was.

'Oh, all right, party-pooper. Let's go.'

Together they went in to see Chelsea, who still had dark, sunken eyes, who still greeted them with monosyllabic tones, but who had the atlas opened out on the bedside table and was studying it intently. Above all, the drip was still in her arm, providing the much needed nutrients her body required.

An hour later, after much discussion and laughter, Eden and David exited Chelsea's room, Eden leaving the photographs for Chelsea to pore over.

'She's kept the drip in.' Eden was elated as David wrote in Chelsea's notes. 'You need to have a meeting with her parents, her siblings, anyone who has a positive influence on her or that she's in regular contact with. No one is to ask her, "How are you doing?" No one is to talk to her about food or her illness or anything of the sort. Organise a meeting with the specialists she's seen, and let them all know that this child has a passion to travel.'

'Think it will make a difference?' David looked up, marvelling at the brightness in Eden's face. She really was stunning. Her eyes radiated brilliance, her hair was bouncing around her shoulders in perfectly formed curls, and her mouth was curved in such a way that he found it difficult to resist kissing it. However, resist he did.

He'd wanted to ask her if she'd dreamt about him last night, because *his* dreams had seemed to feature her all night long. He was losing his focus, forgetting the reasons why he couldn't get involved with her, and being drawn in, held captive by this woman he knew he loved.

'The drip is still in her arm. Small steps, David. Now, where's the footage from Dart's room? Maybe his sleeping patterns might be able to tell us something.'

'Or at least give us a clue.'

'Exactly.'

David collected the tape from where Francie had left it on the desk, and took Eden to a small room where a TV and video-player were set up. The room was no bigger than a broom closet, but it wasn't until they were sitting down side by side that he realised just how small the room was.

'We're in the process of going digital,' he remarked as they waited for the machinery to warm up and for the tape to rewind.

'Hey—this is state-of-the-art compared to what I'm used to working with.'

He smiled at that, trying not to be so aware of her. 'I guess it is.'

'If *we* want to monitor a patient at night we just sit there watching them all night long, trying not to fall asleep,' she half joked as they continued to wait for the tape to rewind. The sensual awareness between them was heightening with each passing moment.

'Small room,' he grumbled softly.

'Sorry? What was that?'

'This room.'

'What about it?'

'It's too small.'

'Maybe you could upgrade that, too.'

'It's you.'

She looked at him askance. 'You want to upgrade me as well?'

'This room is too small for the two of us to be in it together.' David said the words slowly and clearly, and Eden's smile widened as he did so. 'Stop looking at me like that.'

'Like what?' She fluttered her eyelashes at him again.

'You know exactly what I'm talking about.'

'Fancy a quick kiss and cuddle? No one will know. They think we're working.' Eden reached out a hand and touched his arm, sliding her fingers down his crisp cotton shirt until her fingers laced with his. 'I dreamt about you last night and this morning. In fact, I think I'm dreaming right now.'

David swallowed. 'Eden.' Her name was a breathless whisper, and she could feel him beginning to capitulate as his gaze fixated on her mouth. She parted her lips and slipped her tongue out, running it along her upper lip, hoping to make him crack.

He leaned in closer, about to give in completely, ready to give her the kiss he'd been longing to give her from the instant she'd walked onto the ward this morning, when the tape machine clicked noisily, making them jerk back.

'Right. Here we go.' He sat up straighter in his chair, but was sort of pleased when Eden didn't let go of his hand. 'Hopefully we'll discover some answers.'

The tape started playing, the picture coming up on the screen showing the inside of Room 2. Dart's bed was well in focus, and Mrs Wilman's camp bed set up beside it. Nothing much happened, and David flicked a switch, putting the tape into fast-forward mode.

'It's easier to watch like this, otherwise we'll be here all day.'

Eden nodded, looking intently at the pictures playing out before them. Nurses came in, doing observations, ensuring Dart was settled. Everything looked fine. Normal. She frowned, trying to see if they were missing anything, and then it happened.

'Stop the—' She didn't have to say anything more.

David had already pressed the button to slow the tape down to normal speed. Both of them stared open-mouthed at what they saw, Eden's heart breaking for the four-year-old.

The screen showed Mrs Wilman fiddling with Dart's drip. It looked as though she was slowing it down, or stopping it completely. Then she handed him his drinking cup, urging him to drink. Without complaint, without emotion, the child took the cup and drank. His eyes were bleak and lifeless, as though he knew it was pointless to refuse.

'What's in that cup?' Eden was out of her chair in an instant, David not far behind her. 'You distract her. I'll get the cup.'

'What? Eden! *Wait.*'

'Just call her out of the room. Show her Dart's MRI scans. I want that cup and I want it *now.*'

Eden marched into Room 2, pasting an over-bright smile on her face. 'Good morning. I've just come to check on Dart.'

'The nurse has just been round,' Mrs Wilman ventured.

There it was. The drinking cup was beside the bed, in full view of all and sundry. It was innocuous, normal, didn't look at all out of place. Eden was seething inside as she looked at the sick little boy. Sodium. David had said his sodium levels were up. Too much sodium could cause dehydration, stomach pains, elevated blood pressure and a lot of the other symptoms Dart had been admitted with.

She *had* to get that cup!

CHAPTER EIGHT

'SALT water.' Eden had the cup in the small kitchenette. She'd tipped some of the contents out onto a spoon and tasted it as David walked in. 'It's salt. That's why he has excess sodium.'

'You shouldn't taste it!' David removed the cup. 'Anything could be in there. It could be a poisonous substance. We need to wait for Pathology. It'll only take an hour or so.'

'Where I come from pathology takes weeks on end to come back. I knew the contents couldn't be too bad, and besides, Dart's been drinking it non-stop. One tiny teaspoonful wasn't going to hurt me. And now we know. It's salt water.'

'But why? *Why* would any mother do this to her child?'

'Munchausen's Syndrome by proxy.'

'Attention? Mrs Wilman wants attention?'

'Usually it's a parent who is alone who needs

attention—likes the company of the nursing staff, the hospital environment. They'll go to extreme lengths—even allowing their child to have unnecessary surgery—in order to get the attention they crave, for people to listen to them, to respect them.'

'Her husband does work abroad a lot. He's rarely home.'

'Didn't you or someone else mention that she'd only spent one night away from Dart?'

David's eyes widened as everything seemed to fall into place. 'That was the night he picked up.'

'And what happened when she returned?'

'I told her Dart was doing so well we'd be able to discharge him.'

'That meant taking her son home to an empty house where she'd have sole responsibility for him.'

'And then he went downhill again.' David rubbed his fingers across his brow. 'She's a sick woman.'

'She needs help, David.'

He slowly shook his head. 'Not the day I had planned, but…' He straightened his shoulders. 'Duty calls, and that little boy needs rescuing.'

'Let's go save our little musketeer.'

* * *

Quite a few hours had passed before Eden was able to get time to see Sasha, and when she walked into her friend's room she was met with a beaming smile.

'I stood!'

'What?' Eden was by Sasha's side in an instant.

'I stood. All by myself. Well, I was holding onto the parallel bars for dear life, but I still stood.'

'Parallel bars, eh? Practising for the Olympics?'

Sasha laughed with glee. 'Who knows?' They both laughed. 'I *stood*.'

'Does Robert know?'

'He was there. He said he was going out to buy me a new outfit to wear tonight.'

'And so he should. Good man. Wow! This is just the good news I needed.'

'Tough day?'

'And then some. I won't bore you with the details.'

'I've tried calling David, but I've only been able to leave messages for him to call me back.'

'He's still in meetings.'

'It *does* sound like a tough day.'

'But when you *do* tell him it'll bring the smile

back to his face. We both knew you had it in you to kick those statistics which said you'd never walk again right out of the park. Literally.' Tears of happiness pricked behind Eden's eyes. 'It's fantastic. I'm so proud of you.' The two friends hugged.

'And what about you? David told me this morning when he stopped by that you went to see your family yesterday.'

'Yes.' Eden sighed. 'Not as exciting as what you've accomplished.'

'It's still a big deal, Ede. David said it went well?'

She shrugged. 'Todd's still mad, but for the most part it wasn't as bad as I thought it would be. David was incredibly supportive. I wouldn't have managed without him there to hold my hand.'

'Literally?'

Sasha raised her eyebrows and Eden decided not to answer that question…just yet. Although she was excited about the kisses she and David had shared, for some reason, she wasn't ready to blurt it all out to Sasha. Her friend had enough to deal with, and at this stage Eden wasn't even sure what *was* happening between herself and David. She didn't want to give Sasha false hope.

'I'm just so sorry I couldn't have been there for you.'

'Well, you had a good excuse.'

'So…did anything else happen?'

'With my family? Not really.'

'No, with David, you ninny.'

'Why do you ask?' Eden perched herself on a chair next to the bed and tried to look nonchalant.

'Because David looked happy and exhausted and confused this morning, and the last time I saw him look that way was the morning after you two first got together.'

'Oh? So you think because he looked like that this morning we might have…kissed?'

'Yes.' Sasha was immediately on edge, and when Eden didn't say anything straight away, her impatience won out. 'Well? *Did* you?'

Eden couldn't contain her repressed excitement any longer, and a grin split her face as she sighed romantically. 'Yes.'

'Yay!' Sasha clapped her hands. 'This *is* good. This is *brilliant*. My brother and my best friend! Ooh, you can finally marry him and we'll be sisters for real.'

'Whoa. Slow down there, Tex. We just kissed. There are still hurdles to jump.'

'Why didn't you tell me this morning when we spoke? You've had a crush on him, like, for ever, so why the tight lips?'

Eden grimaced. 'I don't know. You've got your whole rehab thing going on, and he's your brother, and—'

'And you didn't want me getting my hopes up and getting all excited and saying that we could finally be real sisters and stuff like that? Right?'

Eden smiled at her friend and squeezed her hand. 'Something like that. Gee, I've missed you.'

'Then stay. You don't have to miss me. You can work things out with David and live the happily-ever-after life I know you've always wanted. You can still travel, still work with PMA. But live here in Sydney. Spend time mending fences with your family.' Sasha nodded enthusiastically. 'You can do this, Eden. It would be great. Our kids can be friends and go to the same schools, create absolute havoc the way we used to.'

'You make a convincing argument.' Eden eased back into the chair as Sasha leaned back on her pillows and sighed again. 'But how about we just focus on getting you rested up so we can celebrate your accomplishments this evening?'

'There is much to celebrate.'

'Yes, there is—which means it's time for you to zip your lip and have a rest.'

'I'm not that tired,' Sasha protested, trying to smother a yawn.

'Like I'm really going to believe you. Shh, and do as the doctor says.'

'You're not *my* doctor.'

'Then do as your best friend says.'

'Oh. All right then, bossy britches.'

Eden picked up the book which was by the bed and started reading out loud from the novel. By the time she'd finished the end of the first page Sasha was asleep. She read on silently to herself, getting so drawn into the story she didn't hear the door open.

'Excuse me?' a soft female voice said from the doorway.

Eden looked up to see a pretty blonde with blue eyes standing there. She was pregnant, and by Eden's expert guess had about eight weeks to go. 'Can I help you?'

The woman pointed to the bed, and Eden noticed the large wedding and engagement rings on her left hand. 'I've come to see Sasha, but she's obviously sleeping. I don't want to wake her.'

Eden looked at her friend. 'She'll sleep for another half an hour at least.'

'Oh.' The blonde looked disappointed. 'I knew I should have called first, but I thought visiting hours were all day on the spinal ward.'

'They are, but patients sleep when they need to. I'm Eden, by the way,' she said, standing up and putting the book down. 'Come and have a seat.'

'*The* Eden?'

'Um…' She was a little stunned at such a question. 'I guess so.'

'I've heard so much about you over the years. Both David and Sasha speak so highly of you.'

Eden raised her eyebrows at this news. So who *was* this woman?

'I'm Jacquie.' Jacquie held out her hand, but as she did so she grimaced and immediately felt her stomach. 'I'm sorry. Alyce has decided to do aerobics all day long, it seems.'

So *this* was Jacqueline. The woman who had married David and later divorced him. Eden kept her smile in place, feeling a little awkward. After all, last night she'd realised she was in love with this woman's ex-husband. Surely that was a good enough reason to feel uncomfortable?

'Alyce?'

'My daughter.' Jacquie rubbed her stomach with pride and joy.

'Come and sit down.' Eden helped Jacquie over to the chair.

'That's right—you're a doctor, too, aren't you? I remember David telling me that. It was a shame you didn't make it back for Sasha's wedding. He was really looking forward to seeing you.'

'I didn't realise I'd be so badly missed,' Eden replied, watching the woman closely, her professional instincts kicking in. 'How long has Alyce been doing her aerobic routine?'

Jacquie shifted uncomfortably. 'For at least the last five hours. I woke up to her doing this, and as I couldn't sleep I thought I'd get up and make my way in here. Everything takes so long. To shower, to dress, and now I've had back pain to top it all off.'

'Have you eaten anything?'

Jacquie laughed. 'You doctors. You simply can't resist. Yes, I've had some dry crackers and a cup of peppermint tea. Alyce likes it.'

'And the back pain?'

'It's fine. *I'm* fine. Worry about Sasha. I'm not due for another eight weeks.'

'Babies come when they're ready, Jacquie, regardless of the schedules we like to impose on them. We only do that so we feel like we have some control over the situation—because if we admit that we don't, we don't usually cope very well.'

Jacquie tilted her head to the side. 'What sort of doctor *are* you?'

Eden smiled. 'I'm a paediatrician, like David, but I've delivered my fair share of babies.' And something told her all was not well with Jacquie. 'When did you last see your obstetrician?'

'Last week. He said I was fine. He said Alyce was fine.'

'And you're due to see him again when?'

'Not until the end of next week.'

'This is your first pregnancy, right?'

Jacquie's gaze dropped, but she answered softly, with a hint of pride. 'Yes. She's been a long time coming, has my beautiful baby.'

'Well, in that case, and for my peace of mind, would you mind seeing your doctor today? Please?'

'You're making a mountain out of molehill.'

Jacquie was starting to get agitated, and Eden didn't blame her. However, Eden's intuition—

both as a woman and as a medical professional—was telling her there was something wrong with this situation. Alyce's 'aerobics' might be a symptom of something else…something else like the onset of early labour.

'Stay there. I'll just get you a glass of water.' Eden walked out of the room and quickly went to the staff kitchenette. One of the nurses was sitting in there, eating her lunch. 'Sorry to disturb. Sasha has a pregnant visitor who looks a little hot to me.' She poured a glass of iced water from the water-cooler and then glanced across at the nurse. 'You don't mind if I borrow a sphygmomanometer and possibly a thermometer?'

'Is Sasha all right?'

'She's fine. It's her visitor. Just being an over-protective doctor, that's all.'

'OK. The equipment you need will be at the nurses' station. It'll give you her vitals. Let me know if you need any help.'

'Thanks.' Eden returned to Sasha's room, wheeling in the electronic sphygmo machine. It was one of the new ones, with all the bells and whistles. 'Here you are,' she said, and handed the glass to Jacquie. 'Sip it slowly.'

'What's that for?' Jacquie asked. 'Does Sasha need some tests?'

'It's not for Sasha. I'm sorry if I'm being forward and pushy, Jacquie, especially as we've only just met, but do you mind if I take your blood pressure? Just to check it. You look rather flushed to me.'

Jacquie dabbed at her forehead with a handkerchief. 'I'll be fine. The water is doing the trick.'

Eden shrugged. 'Humour me.'

'You *are* a real doctor, aren't you? You're not just making it up?'

'I'm a trained doctor.' Eden held out the blood pressure cuff. 'Please?'

'Oh, all right, then,' she reluctantly agreed, and allowed Eden to wind the cuff around her arm. The machine did its job and Eden frowned.

'Your blood pressure is definitely elevated, Jacquie.' Before there was any room for protest, she clipped the oximeter onto Jacquie's index finger. When that reading came back, Eden's frown intensified. 'Who's your obstetrician? You should call him or her straight away.'

'Why? There's nothing wrong with me.'

'I beg to differ. Do you have the name and number? I'll call.'

Jacquie frowned. 'He's probably busy. He and

his family are highly respected, I'll have you know. His father delivered me, and so it's only right that I have his son deliver my child.'

'That's just fine and dandy, but it's his job to be interrupted when one of his patients needs him. His name?'

Jacquie reluctantly told Eden the information. Eden crossed to the phone by Sasha's bedside and asked the ladies on the switchboard to have the obstetrician call her immediately. Once that was done, she called the paediatric ward and spoke to Francie.

'I know David's busy, but hopefully by now he can leave Mrs Wilman with the social workers,' she stated to the nurse. 'I need him up here in Sasha's room.'

'Yes,' Jacquie interjected haughtily. 'Ask David to come here. He'll sort this out. You're being highly unreasonable, Eden—especially as we've just met.'

Eden ignored the pregnant woman and focused on what Francie was saying.

'Is Sasha all right?' There was concern in the nurse's tone.

'Sash is fine. Either ask David to call me or to come if he can—'

'Wait, Eden. He's just come out of Room 2.'

Eden waited, and a second later David's voice came down the line. She ignored the way his smooth tones affected her.

'Eden?'

'David. I'm in Sasha's room. Would you mind coming here and bringing a foetal heart monitor with you?'

'What? Why? Sasha's not pregnant.'

'I know that. Jacquie's here.'

He was silent for a moment. 'The baby.' The words were a whisper. 'You think there's something wrong?'

'I do.'

'Right. I'm on my way.'

'Is he coming?' Jacquie asked, her chin still raised in a haughty manner.

'Yes.' Eden replaced the receiver as Sasha began to stir. 'Oh, I'm sorry,' Eden said softly to her friend. 'I didn't mean to wake you—and you haven't slept for all that long.'

Sasha yawned. 'It's all right. Plenty of time to rest. What's going on?'

'Jacquie's come to visit.' Eden pointed across to where Jacquie was sitting.

'Is David coming?' Jacquie asked again.

There was no fear in her tone, but it held a lot of impatience.

'Yes. Just sit there. I'll be right back.' Eden dashed out to the nurses' station once more and found a tempanic thermometer.

'What now?' Jacquie asked when Eden returned.

'Please?' Eden put a gentle hand on the other woman's shoulder. 'Relax. It won't take but a moment.'

'I know how long it takes. I have had my temperature taken before.'

The thermometer beeped. 'Thirty-eight. You're not leaving this hospital.'

'Are you completely out of your mind?' Jacquie asked, and turned to Sasha. 'I only wanted to come and visit you, but I see now that I was wrong to do so while this crazy woman is here.'

'You think something is wrong?' Sasha asked Eden.

'Yes.'

Sasha turned to Jacquie, who was shifting forward in the chair as though she were about to stand up. 'Please, Jacquie,' she implored. 'Listen to Eden. She knows about these things.'

'Sasha is right,' David said as he stalked into the room. 'Eden has amazing instincts.'

She might have amazing instincts, but she could also turn to a boneless mass of jelly just from hearing his voice. She pulled herself together and looked at him with thanks.

He didn't like it when she looked at him like that—as though she wanted to wind her body around his and never let go. The uncanny thing was, he wanted to do exactly the same thing to her. Instead, he forced himself to look away and focused his attention on his ex-wife. 'Good afternoon, Jacqueline.'

He handed Eden the foetal heart monitor she'd requested, before crossing to Jacquie's side and pressing a polite kiss to her cheek. It was the same greeting Eden had seen him giving his mother over the years, and she realised that the protocols of high society were still maintained as far as he was concerned. It was, however, interesting to note that he treated Jacquie with such polite indifference.

'Report?' He turned to look at Eden, and she snapped back into doctor mode.

'BP and temperature elevated, swelling of the feet and hands.' She unwound the heart monitor and plugged it in. 'She's thirty-three weeks. I've put in a call to her obstetrician.'

David knelt down. 'I'm just going to check your feet,' he said to Jacquie, and pressed carefully. 'Is Gray your obstetrician?' he asked.

'Yes.'

'I'll make sure he's here. Don't you worry about it.' A moment later, he said, 'These shoes are coming off.' He removed them and set them aside. 'What's your husband's phone number?' He pulled a piece of paper and a pen from his pocket.

'What *is* going on?' Jacquie demanded, looking at the three people in the room. 'Have you all gone stark raving mad? I'm just a little hot. That's normal when a woman is pregnant. The books say so.'

'Yes,' David said softly but firmly, 'but not as hot as you are. It's not good for the baby. What's Paul's number, Jacqueline?'

Jacquie looked at him for a moment, before rattling off her husband's contact number.

David turned to Eden. 'I'll organise for her admission to Maternity.'

'Thanks. Much appreciated.'

She smiled at him, her green eyes alive with appreciation and sincerity. David stood where he was for a whole five seconds, simply staring at her, unable to believe just how dynamic and beautiful she was. The sunbeams from the window were shining into the room, highlighting the glorious colours of Eden's hair and giving her skin a golden tinge which only made her even more desirable. He could quite easily lose himself in this woman. She was so magnetic—especially when she looked at him as she was doing now.

'David?' It was Sasha who spoke, who broke the moment he and Eden were sharing.

'Hmm? Right. Yes. I've got things to do.'

With that, he left the room, and Eden sucked in a deep breath to get herself back on track. Honestly, when he looked at her the way he just had, her body turned to mush and her brain could think of nothing but the way his arms felt around her. Strong, sure and steady.

After David had gone, Eden strapped the foetal heart monitor around Jacquie's middle and positioned the instrument correctly. A moment later the readings started coming through. 'You're having minor contractions,' Eden reported.

'What? But I can't feel anything.' Jacquie stared at the monitor Eden was watching.

'They're very small, but things are happening.'

'But I'm only thirty-three weeks! Alyce can't come yet.'

'I hate to break this to you again, Jacquie, but as I said, babies come when they're ready. Unless we can stop your labour, Alyce is on her way.'

Jacquie clutched at Eden's hand, her eyes wild. 'But she's not ready. It's not time.'

Eden watched the desperate reaction of the mother-to-be, and although most women who went into premature labour were scared and frightened, she sensed there was something else going on. 'This *is* your first pregnancy?'

'I miscarried two last year, but they were both within the first six weeks.'

Eden nodded. 'You've had trouble getting pregnant?'

'Yes. For years. You have to *do* something.'

'I am.'

'Eden?' David called, poking his head around the door. 'Can I see you for a moment?'

She nodded and crossed to where he was standing, just outside Sasha's room. 'What's the problem?'

'I've managed to get hold of Gray and he's on his way. He's a good doctor, but as far as the baby's care goes I'd like you to do it.'

'Me?' Eden wasn't sure she wanted to be looking after a baby belonging to David's ex-wife.

'Well, *I* can't do it. Although Jacquie and I are friends, it just doesn't seem…right.'

She spread her arms wide. 'You have other colleagues—and Jacquie has her own private obstetrician practically on retainer! Surely the son of the son of the man who looked after her when she was born is all set to look after her baby?'

David grinned at her words. 'Doctors don't work like that, and you know it,' he remarked, even though he knew Eden had been joking. 'She has chosen a paediatrician—'

'Who is no doubt socially acceptable?' Eden interjected.

'But he is off on compassionate leave at the moment,' David continued.

'I just hate society and its socially acceptable forms of how things should be done,' she grumbled.

'You only hate it because you were so restricted by it,' he soothed, rubbing a hand up and down her arm. 'Other people *need* rules and regulations. They find it comforting.'

'Only because it gives them strict guidelines on what's expected of them in life. No one should have their life *that* meticulously planned.

It's just wrong—and it also means there are too many people in this world not reaching their full potential as human beings—'

David placed a finger over her lips and leaned closer. 'I would have preferred to kiss you to shut you up,' he murmured, his tone deep. 'Your eyes flash with fire when you get into one of your rants, and you lift your chin in that defiant way I've seen you do so often. It's very, very sexy, Eden. Lord knows I'd love you to continue—if for no other reason than I'd get to admire you—but time is of the essence, and right now I need you focused.'

He left his finger in place for a fraction of a second longer…long enough for Eden to wet it with the tip of her tongue. He jerked it back and she smiled. 'How do you expect me to focus when you say things like that?'

'I expect you to focus because you're a professional.'

'Yes. Right. I am.' She cleared her throat and he took a step back, giving them both a bit more air, a bit more room to move.

'Now, as I was saying, I'd like *you* to be Jacquie's paediatrician. Because even though she's my ex-wife I know how important this child is to her, and there's no one I trust as much as you.'

Eden watched his mouth as he spoke, trying not to be mesmerised by him. When she realised he'd finished, she looked at his eyes and saw that he was waiting for her to respond. 'All right. I'll do it. For *you*. But I'm sure Jacquie won't like it. I don't think I'm her favourite person at the moment.'

His smile was filled with gratitude. 'She'll come around to you. Everyone always does…in the end.'

Everyone except his parents, but she didn't really care about them. 'Gee, thanks.'

'You know what I mean.'

'I do.'

'Thank you, Eden. It shouldn't take too much to convince Jacquie. She always insists on the best, and that's exactly what you are. The best.' David met her gaze and held it for a moment, and she wondered whether he was talking about her medical skills or something else.

'Flattery will get you everywhere, Dr Montgomery.' She looked up and saw the orderlies getting out of the lift, pushing a vacant barouche.

'This way,' David instructed them, and headed into Sasha's room—where they found that Sasha had been talking sense to Jacquie and the expectant mother was now more than willing to be whisked away to the maternity ward.

David and Eden stayed with Jacquie until Dr Gray arrived. Eden vaguely remembered him from the social set, but he remembered her completely.

'Staged a protest against your own father's company. How could anyone forget that?' Dr Gray shook hands with Eden. 'I always admired you for standing up for what you believed in.'

'Really? Uh…well, thanks.'

'In fact, I remembered your determination when *my* father wanted to push me into studying law instead of medicine. It helped me to take a stand and head in the direction I preferred.' Dr Gray was busy checking the readings from the foetal heart monitor as he spoke.

'Wow.' Eden blinked and looked across at David, who was leaning against the cupboard, his arms folded across his chest. He nodded as though he, too, was impressed with what Dr Gray had shared. 'I'm…uh…glad I was able to help—even if I didn't realise I was.'

'Excuse me,' Jacquie remarked, that haughty tone at perfect pitch, 'can we focus on *me*, please? I *am* apparently in labour.'

'Yes, of course.' Dr Gray turned his full attention to his patient, and wasn't at all happy with the observation readings the nurse reported. 'Your blood pressure is increasing, Jacquie, and that means the baby's heart-rate is decelerating.' He turned to the nurse. 'IV line and oxygen, stat. Blood test, a.s.a.p. We need to rule out infection.'

Eden helped Dr Gray move Jacquie onto her side.

'Wh-what's going on?' Jacquie asked, her voice quivering.

'I'll explain in a minute, Jacquie,' Dr Gray soothed. A moment later the foetal monitor gave a better read-out and they all sighed. 'Sorry about that. Didn't mean to scare you.'

'Well, you did—and why is Eden still here. David?'

'Eden's going to be your paediatrician,' David explained walking to Jacquie's side so she could see him more easily instead of having to crane her neck.

'But I had it planned. It was *all* planned. This wasn't supposed to happen today. Everything is wrong. This isn't the way I had it planned.'

'Shh,' Dr Gray soothed her. 'You need to calm down. Deep breaths, Jacquie.'

'Dr Gray's right,' said David, calmly explaining why Jacquie's appointed paediatrician couldn't make it. 'Eden will look after your baby because in my opinion she's the best there is. You want the best for your baby, don't you?'

'Alyce. Her name is Alyce.'

David nodded, his voice gentle. 'Alyce is important to you, and therefore you need the best care you can get. The best is Eden.'

'What about Paul?'

'He's on his way,' Dr Gray informed her.

'We'll leave you to get some rest,' Eden said. They walked out of the room, Dr Gray not far behind them, leaving Jacquie in the care of two well-trained nurses.

'Jacquie's definitely displaying all the signs and symptoms of pre-eclampsia. Good pick-up, David.' He gave his colleague a manly pat on the back.

'It was Eden.'

'Ah. In that case, well done, Eden. I take it you're staying in Sydney?'

'For a while.' Eden smiled up at David. 'I've only been here a few days, and David already has me working.'

'I didn't want you to be bored.'

'More like you needed my help.'

'And I know how much you love to help.'

'Whatever the reason,' Dr Gray said, feeling as though he was watching a tennis match—a tennis match with a lot of sensual undercurrents, 'I'm glad he's persuaded you. I've read a few of your papers. Incredible stuff.'

'Thank you. Anyway, we'll leave you to it. If you need me, I think it'll be best if you page David. If I'm not with him, he'll know where to find me.'

'OK.' Dr Gray headed back to Jacquie's room and Eden looked at David.

'Time for a cuppa, methinks.' They headed towards the hospital cafeteria. 'What a day!'

'You're not wrong.'

'How did things go with Mrs Wilman?'

David gave her a rundown on what had happened with social services and the psychiatric consult he'd called in. 'Dart, thankfully, is now responding to treatment.'

'That *is* good news.' They got their drinks and sat at a table. 'Oh, and Sash has good news, too. She forgot to tell you, what with all the extra goings-on.'

'What is it?'

'Ah…I'm not ruining it for her. Just make

sure you stop in and see her on your way back
to the ward.'

'Will do.'

Eden took a sip of her coffee, regarding him
closely. 'David, can I ask you something?'

He laughed ironically. 'Have you ever been
stopped before?'

'Well, it's personal. It's about you and Jacquie,
but I don't want you to think I'm prying.'

'Oh. Right.' He braced himself. 'What's the
question?'

'When you were married, did she have any
miscarriages?'

'No.' His answer was immediate.

'You're sure?'

'Yes.' He clenched his jaw for a moment, then
swallowed. 'Why do you ask?'

'She said she had two last year, and I was just
wondering whether there's something else
wrong. Is there a virus attacking her babies? Are
the blood types of mother and foetus different?
That sort of thing.'

'I don't know anything about her miscarriages.'

'And you two didn't try to have any children?
Didn't plan any?'

David clenched his jaws together. 'Bringing children into a marriage that should never have happened in the first place didn't seem like the wisest of ideas.'

Eden was a little surprised at his reaction, and also a little confused. She would have sworn that Jacquie had said she'd been trying to have a child for a very long time. But David obviously didn't want to talk to her about his marriage, and she could understand that. 'OK. Well, I'm sure Dr Gray knows what's going on and has everything under control. I'm just trying to play through a few different scenarios in my mind. You know— be prepared for when the baby arrives.'

'Is that all?' He pushed his half-empty cup away and stood.

'Yes.'

'I need to go.'

He was gone so fast Eden didn't have time to blink or even to call out his name. She'd obviously been treading on some very thin ice, but she wasn't sure what on earth she'd said to offend him.

CHAPTER NINE

AN HOUR later Eden was in Sasha's room when a call came through from David to say that Dr Gray needed her.

'Apparently, a second urine sample has come back showing traces of uric-acid and protein,' David informed her.

'He's going to induce the labour?' she stated.

'I would presume so.'

'OK. Thanks. I'll head to Maternity now to check on things.' She was about to ask him if he was all right, but found that he'd already hung up the phone and she was listening to the dial tone. Something was wrong, and while she wanted to go and find him and get him to tell her exactly what was bothering him, she decided to give him some space.

When she arrived in Jacquie's room she realised that Paul, Jacquie's husband, had arrived and was busy pacing up and down, not bothering to keep out of the staff's way. Dr Gray had already set up a magnesium drip, which would help reduce the swelling in Jacquie's limbs, and a catheter bag hung beside the bottom of the bed.

He was intent on trying all the options, as Jacquie wanted to have a natural birth, but three hours later things had become steadily worse.

Eden had spent those hours forcing herself to keep away from David, yet all the while trying to figure out what had made him so touchy towards her. What had she done wrong? Was she not supposed to discuss his past marriage with him? She hadn't meant anything by her questions—it had been purely for medical reasons she'd asked them.

Now, though, she needed to concentrate, and she reluctantly pushed thoughts of her delicious David to the back of her mind.

'We've tried the Cytotec and it hasn't worked,' Dr Gray was explaining. 'We've tried the Foley bulb, and still you're only three centimetres dilated. Your waters have broken, and although that's brought you a bit of relief it's made things worse for Alyce.'

'Dr Gray's right,' Eden confirmed. 'Alyce is compressing her cord because there's no fluid to keep the pressure off. This means her heart-rate is decelerating faster and she's not recovering as well as she was before. To top it all off, you're exhausted. Even if you dilated the full ten centimetres in the next hour, there's no way you would have the energy to push a baby out. It's not your fault,' Eden added, seeing the tears trickle down her patient's cheeks. 'It's just the way things are. What's important now is to get Alyce out, and quickly.'

'My wife wants to have her child naturally,' Paul stated firmly, glaring at Eden with total distrust, as though she was responsible for what was happening to his wife.

'Paul, be reasonable,' Dr Gray said. He was a sweet, passive man, not at all comfortable with the confrontation Paul seemed intent on starting.

David walked into the room at that point and came to stand by Eden. 'Problem?' He nodded to Jacquie's husband. 'Paul.'

'What Jacquie wants, she gets,' Paul said. 'If she wants to have this baby naturally, that's exactly what's going to happen—or I'll be suing not only the three of you, but the hospital as well. My family and my company make very important donations to this institution, and as such I demand my wife receives not only the treatment she desires, but that everything goes smoothly.'

David could see Dr Gray looked ready to pass out at being spoken to in such a way. But Eden, it seemed, was on the other end of the scale, and about to bubble over with anger. It would be up to him to keep the situation calm and under control.

'I understand, Paul.' His voice was smooth but firm, brooking no argument. 'However, as a successful businessman, you may want to weigh up your options a bit more. If it is deemed necessary to administer an epidural, for either pain relief or surgical needs, then that's what will happen, regardless of Jacqueline's wishes, and I'll tell you why.'

Paul glared at David, and Eden realised that although Jacquie and David may have divorced amicably that same polite friendship didn't apply to Jacquie's present husband. 'I'm waiting.'

'Because you want your wife and daughter to live.' David's words were spoken clearly and calmly, laced heavily with sincerity.

Paul scoffed. 'You're over-dramatising things.'

'No. We're informing you of the risks. Pre-eclampsia is a very real risk—not only to your daughter's health, but to your wife's as well. As doctors we take our patient's health seriously, and we do whatever it takes to save lives. If that means urging Jacqueline to have a Caesarean section, then so be it. You can't always get what you want, and it's time both of you started to think of your baby rather than yourselves. You're going to become parents, which means there will be a little girl who will need you to consider *her* needs before any personal or society wants.' He glanced at Eden briefly. 'That's just the way things are now, and I strongly urge you to listen to Dr Gray's and Eden's recommendations.'

'You're just trying to scare her,' Paul retaliated, although it was clear that the wind had definitely been taken out of his sails. 'All of you.'

'Believe me,' Eden said, more calm now thanks to David stepping in when he had. 'It's not my practice either to lie to my patients or to scare them into treatment. You're being given honest medical recommendations, taking into consideration Jacquie's and Alyce's well-being. The ultimate decision is yours, but the longer you wait the less chance Alyce will have of fighting once she's born. She's eight weeks early and she needs all the strength she can get.'

'We'll give you a few minutes to talk it over,' Dr Gray remarked, and the three doctors headed out of the room.

'Thanks.' Dr Gray held out his hand to David. 'I was so shocked by what he was saying, I was just…' He shrugged.

'Flabbergasted?' Eden provided.

'Exactly.'

'I was livid.' She smiled at David, unsure of the reception she'd receive from him. 'Just as well Mr Cool, Calm and Collected stepped in.'

David merely nodded at her words, but didn't return her smile. That wasn't good. It meant something was really wrong—but what?

'I need to get back to the ward. Call me if I'm needed.' He couldn't stand there looking at Eden's bewildered eyes any longer. He knew he should explain, tell her why he was acting the way he was, but it was hardly the time and place to let her know the truth. Her questions about his marriage had thrown him completely. He could understand why she'd asked them, knew it was for medical reasons alone, but in that instant he'd been swamped not only with the failure of his marriage but with the fact that he'd never have the children he'd wished for.

He headed off, feeling her gaze upon him. He turned at the top of the corridor to look back at her. 'By the way—you do have good malpractice insurance, right?'

She smiled at his words, the pressure on her heart lifting a little at his question. 'Why? Are you offering to share?'

He returned her smile before walking off, and it was a much happier Eden who returned to her work of helping Dr Gray.

Twenty minutes later Jacquie was being wheeled round to Theatre, and after having an epidural block administered, Dr Gray began the C-section. David was in the room, near Eden. She couldn't see him, but she could feel him. Her body seemed to know exactly where he was at all times during the short but successful operation.

Once Paul had cut the cord, and Alyce had been shown to Jacquie, Eden took over. She performed the baby's observations, shaking her head at the poor APGAR score. She put an oximetry probe on the small foot, which would check the baby was receiving the correct amount of oxygen. Next she put in an umbilical venous catheter, as well as an arterial catheter, and finally a nasogastric tube so the little girl could be fed.

They transferred Alyce to the NICU, and although Eden was the doctor treating the little girl, she was pleased David was nearby if for no other reason than to give her strength. He had become a very important lifeline to her, and it was one she never wanted to let go.

'Give her a bolus dose of ten percent dextrose,' Eden ordered the nurses. 'And check her sugar levels again. Her lungs are stiff, so administer surfactant via syringe before turning on the ventilator.'

'What are you doing?' Paul demanded, coming up behind Eden and almost scaring her. David turned to face him, and Eden saw the mask of the professional in place. Any arguments Paul had were about to be overruled.

'We're making sure your daughter can breathe properly. Even though Dr Gray was able to get quite a few doses of steroids into Jacquie to assist in increasing Alyce's lung function, it still wasn't enough,' David said.

'Alyce's lungs are stiff,' Eden continued. 'We need to keep the moisture up around her so she's able to breathe in the necessary amount of oxygen. At the moment her lungs can't expand and contract properly, which isn't a good thing.'

Eden decided she'd had enough of his blustering and bullying. Niceness was something he might not be used to, and catching him off guard might be just what they needed tc keep him quiet.

'Come with me,' she said softly, holding out a hand to him. Paul looked at her hand and backed away as though she were insane.

'What do you want?'

Eden continued to keep her voice as calm as possible. No doubt Paul hadn't had the best of days either. She didn't know what was going on in his life, what had made him the blustering pain that he was, but right now, she could do one thing for him. 'Over here. To the sink. If you wash your hands you can touch her.'

'Touch?'

Eden's smile was warm and genuine, her words soft. 'Alyce. You do want to touch her, don't you? I know what she means to you, Paul. How special this little girl is. Your daughter has arrived. *Your daughter.* You're a daddy.' She smiled as she said the last words, watching the way Paul gaped at her in astonishment. 'Now, wash your hands and go and make first contact. She needs you. Alyce really needs you.'

David watched as Eden calmed the savage beast, and in the next instant Paul had his hand in the humidicrib, rubbing his finger on Alyce's cheek. 'She's so…tiny.'

Eden smiled. 'Enjoy it while you can. Before you know it she'll be running up your credit card bills and borrowing your BMW.'

Paul smiled, and it completely changed his face.

'We'll give you some privacy, but let me know if you need anything.' Eden took David's hand in hers, nodding to the nurse as they walked by.

'And she does it again.'

'Pardon?' Eden looked up at him as they headed out of the NICU.

'I have never seen that man smile before.'

'He's never been a father before,' Eden returned softly.

David stiffened at her words, and after a moment let go of her hand. His tone, however, was controlled and even. 'You truly have a gift, Eden. You're able to see to the heart of a person and provide them with exactly what they need. Take Chelsea, for example. She's kept the drip in for the past two days and is actually engaging the staff in conversation. Of course, she's asking them all about the travel experiences they've had, but it's better than being the confused child she was when she came in.'

'She's an intelligent girl,' Eden agreed. 'If she'd been older it would have been more difficult to get through to her.'

'But you knew exactly what she needed.'

'No. I saw a spark. I tried something. It worked. That's all, David. Listen, I'm going to go check on Jacquie, and then see Sasha before heading off to get ready for our date tonight.' She stopped at a junction in the corridor.

'Date?'

David's face registered his bewilderment, and she couldn't resist reaching up to stroke his cheek. The poor man had so much on his mind. She wished he'd let her in, trust her enough to tell her what was really bothering him, but she couldn't force him.

'Sasha and Robert? We're having dinner with them tonight.'

'Yes. Yes, I remember now.' He tried not to lean into her hand, but couldn't help himself. Her touch was so comforting, so supportive, and exactly what he needed. Could she read him as well as she could read everyone else? That thought made him step back. 'I'm going to the ward.'

'Right.' She dropped her hand, telling herself she had to be content with the fact that he'd at least accepted the compassion she'd been offering. 'Seven o'clock. Sasha's room.'

He nodded before turning and heading off in the opposite direction. She watched him walk away and wondered if she'd be able to get through to him or whether she would lose him for a second time.

Robert met Eden at the entrance to the hospital. 'Sorry,' she said, getting out of her taxi. 'I'm running late.'

'Fine by me,' Robert said, coming forward to kiss her cheek, a bag in his hand. 'You look fantastic, Eden. David's going to pop a gasket when he sees you.'

She was dressed in a pair of black boots, black trousers, and an emerald-green top which highlighted her vibrant eyes. She carried a black fitted coat over her arm, and funky earrings twirled near her neck. She'd scooped her hair back and up into a simple ponytail, which revealed a decent expanse of skin from her neck to her cleavage.

'Here's hoping,' she laughed. 'So…ready for some fun?'

'Exactly where are we going?' Robert asked when they were in the lift.

'Ahh, a surprise for you as well, I think. You've both been through so much, it's about time you broke free of this institution for a few hours and let loose.'

Robert laughed. 'Sash has told me about some of the crazy things you've done, but I never thought I'd witness any of them, let alone be a part of one.'

The lift doors opened and Eden smiled. 'I'm not planning anything crazy for tonight—sorry to disappoint—but I guarantee you'll have fun.'

'Same thing in my book.'

'What? Fun and crazy? Oh, Robert, dear Robert, you've got a lot to learn. Now, you go to your wife, help her finish getting ready, and I'll be there in a moment. I just have to make a few quick phone calls.'

Eden went to the nurses' desk and called the maternity ward first to check on Jacquie. After receiving a good report, she called through to the NICU.

'How's Alyce doing?' she asked the nurse.

'I was just about to call you, Dr Caplan.'

'Problem?'

'I'd like you to review her. She tried to stop breathing about two minutes ago, but she's a stubborn one. Fighting for her life.'

'I'll be right there.' Eden left a message for the nurse to pass on to Sasha and headed towards the NICU. She opened the door to the stairwell and ran slap-bang into David. His arms came about her, holding both of them steady.

'This is getting to be a habit.'

'One I'd love to continue,' she returned, loving the way he could make her tingle all over. 'Right now, however, I need to see Alyce.'

David's concern was instant. 'Problems?'

Eden explained as the two of them headed to the stairs. When they arrived at the NICU, it was to find all of Alyce's vitals were back in the normal range. Eden checked and rechecked all the tubes and wires, then checked and rechecked the machines—even though she knew the nursing staff would have done their own thorough checks.

Once she was satisfied that Alyce was doing as well as could be expected, they headed back out—but not until she'd made sure the nurses had her cellphone number.

'*I* don't have your cellphone number,' David said as they headed back to Sasha's room.

'That's because you've never asked for it,' she retorted. She could feel his gaze on her as they climbed the stairs and it warmed her through.

'You look lovely,' he ventured when they came to the top of the stairs.

Eden angled her head. 'Lovely? A book can be described as *lovely*.'

'Pretty.'

'Now I'm a little girl with blonde pigtails in a floral dress. Come *on*. Dig a little deeper.'

'Eden. Now is not the time to tease.'

'Why? Why don't you want me to tease?' She eased closer, using the confined area to her advantage. 'Is that what you really want, David? For me to stop?'

He closed his eyes and groaned, placing his hands at her waist and hauling her against him. He looked down into her upturned face. 'You are driving me insane, lady.'

'Getting better,' she murmured, and leaned in to press a feather-light kiss to his lips.

'You're wild and fun and sexy and intoxicating,' he ground out.

'Now you've got the hang of it.' She kissed

him again, revelling in the feel of his body against hers.

'Sasha's waiting,' he whispered against her lips.

'She'll understand,' Eden returned, but knew he had a point. After a few more teasing kisses she shifted back and opened the stairwell door, pleased when he didn't immediately let go of her.

When they walked in to Sasha's room, it was to find her friend tucked warmly into a wheelchair, impatiently waiting.

'There you two are. Right, now, let's get out of here before any emergencies happen or before someone comes and tells me I can't go.'

'You have permission to go,' Eden said as Robert wheeled Sasha's chair out to the lifts.

'I know, yet I still feel as though I'm escaping. Honestly, Ede, being stuck in this place for the past few weeks has started to feel worse than that time we ended up in gaol.'

Robert raised his eyebrows. 'You were in *gaol*?'

Sasha laughed and started to recount the story, and that set the tone for the rest of the night. The four of them enjoyed a lovely meal at a glitzy restaurant. The food was good. The company was better, and they laughed for most of the time.

'How are you feeling?' Eden asked later, as she pressed her fingers to Sasha's wrist to take her pulse. Both she and David had kept close tabs on Sasha's health throughout the night.

'Getting tired.'

'Not surprising,' David dropped a kiss to his sister's head. 'You've done well to make it this far—especially after such an eventful day.' When Sasha had told him that she'd stood up on her own tears had welled in his eyes. In those few words he knew that with hard work and determination his sister would one day walk again. His sister wasn't the sort of person to back down from a challenge. Besides, she'd have himself and Robert to support her throughout the entire ordeal. Would Eden stay for that long? It could take months—even a whole year. Would she stay?

After they'd returned Sasha to the hospital, David took Eden back to her hotel. 'Coffee?' she asked.

David pointed to the hotel lounge area in the lobby. 'Down here? Sure.'

She smiled. 'Not in my room?' She fluttered her eyelashes at him. 'Ooh, David. Why ever not? Is it because you find me wild and fun and sexy?'

'You forgot intoxicating,' he added as he led her to a comfortable lounge chair, making sure he sat opposite her rather than next to her. To be too close to Eden only meant torturing himself even further. 'And that's precisely the reason.'

They ordered drinks and discussed their patients and the exhausting day they'd both had. When David had checked on Dart before coming out this evening, the boy had had colour in his cheeks and was beginning to complain about 'yucky meddy' again.

'And Mrs Wilman?'

David shook his head. 'She's in the psychiatric ward under strict observation tonight. Dart's father has cancelled his business trip and will be here tomorrow morning. He's as astounded about what has happened as everybody else.'

'I hope she gets better. Her condition *can* be helped, so long as she's willing to help herself.'

'Just like Chelsea?'

'Just like any patient. People in general have the ability to work through situations and problems, taking things one step at a time, getting help from counsellors or psychologists or even just talking to a friend. Life is far too short to be wrapped up in the what-ifs and maybes of the world.'

'Is that why you let me pressure you to see your family?'

'You didn't pressure me, David. You supported me. And that's why I knew I needed to see them.' She smiled. 'Sometimes *knowing* and *doing* are very difficult things to combine, but with will-power and support it can be achieved.'

Their drinks were delivered, and David eased back in his chair, looking at her for a moment.

'Why do I get the strange feeling you're talking about me here?'

'I guess I'm not so subtle, eh? There's a cloud hanging over you, David. I'm not saying I know what it is, but it's there, and it's stopping you from moving on with your life.'

'Is this because I've said that things wouldn't ever work out between us?'

'Sort of. You say cryptic things, you don't give me explanations for them, and then you kiss me as though you just can't help yourself.'

'I can't.' He rubbed a hand across his brow, massaging his temple for a moment. 'It's true, though, Eden. It can't work out between us.'

'You need to give me a solid reason why not,

David. I *am* in love with you. I know it for a fact. And although you may not believe me, I am not the sort of girl to fall in love with just anyone.'

'Not Tony or Jett or the plethora of other men you've mentioned?'

'All of them friends. Most of them colleagues. Despite that, it's beside the point—because none of them make me feel the way you do.'

'Eden, we can't. Don't love me. Don't want to be with me.'

'Why not? You told me that I didn't know who I was, that I spent my time helping everyone else and never spent enough time just being myself. Well, I listened to you and I've realised you're right. I didn't know who I was, what I wanted out of life. Of course I'm happy with my job, with helping people, but I do want more.'

'You want marriage and a family.'

'I want *you*.'

'You want what every other woman wants. I can't provide it.' His voice had taken on a coolness she'd never heard before, and for a moment she actually believed *he* believed the words he was saying.

'Just for me, or for any woman?' she asked, determined to keep her voice calm and controlled.

This could turn out to be the most important conversation of her life, and she needed to make sure she didn't blow it. She tried to mask the confusion and hurt she was experiencing.

She thought she'd dealt with the pain of his first rejection, but it was surging back tenfold and she felt as though she was a teenager again, having him tell her to keep her distance and not to pursue him.

'Any woman.'

Eden sighed and felt a weight lift from her. It wasn't just her. She could work with this. 'I've done a lot of soul-searching these past few days—deep soul-searching. I've listened to what you've had to say, I've processed it. And I've made peace with my family and myself with regards to the past.' She pulled her hair from the band and flicked the locks over her shoulder, massaging her scalp a little.

David was mesmerised for a second, just watching her as she pulled her fingers through her gorgeous curls. His mind went blank and he completely lost track of what they'd been discussing. He loosened his tie and undid the top button of his shirt. It was always like that around Eden. He would try to talk sensibly with her, but then she'd distract him and he would become mesmerised by the way her eyes darkened to a deeper shade of green whenever she became passionate about something. Now was no exception, and although she wasn't getting riled up, the emotions were still there… She was just better at controlling it now that she was older.

She was so amazingly attractive he was having a difficult time keeping his breathing even, not to mention his train of thought. He needed to be harsh, to let her see that this time he wasn't going to give in, wasn't going to let her talk him around. It was for her own good.

'I know exactly what I want to do with my life, David, and that in itself is very freeing. It's something I couldn't have done without your help.' She was having difficulty forming the words, especially when he was looking at her as though he was about to toss aside the coffee table which separated them, not caring if drinks got spilt or if he wrecked the lobby. His eyes told her he wanted her, wanted her so badly he was willing to throw all sense and reason out of the window. So how could his mouth say that he didn't want to be with her, that she was better off without him?

'Because you've helped me, because I've taken those boxes out…the ones I'd hidden for so long…because I've looked inside them and really tried to figure things out, I think it's only fair that I return the favour. That I help you figure out what it is that *you* want out of life.'

'I know what I want, Eden.'

'And what's that?'

'Peace.'

She waggled her eyebrows up and down suggestively. 'I can give you peace.'

He laughed without humour. 'You give me anything *but* peace, Eden. You're the one who ties me up in knots, who makes me forget where I am, what I'm doing. Who makes me wild with jealousy if I hear you talk about another man—friend, colleague or otherwise.'

'And why aren't these good things?'

'Because I want peace.'

'Peace is boring. Well…not all the time, but you know what I mean. There needs to be a balance, David, and you're never going to get that until you talk to me—until you can trust me enough to tell me what it is that has you one hundred percent certain that we can never be together.'

'Maybe I just don't love you.'

Eden heard the words, felt them pierce her heart, and then instantly rejected them. 'That's not the case.'

'Are you saying that I *am* in love with you?'

'You must be—otherwise your actions would be far more rational than they are. You love me. I love you. But we also need to trust each other, David. *Please.*'

Her tone was imploring, and before he realised she'd even moved, she'd reached forward and taken his hands in hers. The touch filled him instantly with desire and need. This woman was everything he'd ever wanted and more. It wasn't that he didn't trust her, he did, with every fibre of his being, but he'd known this conversation had to happen at some point.

Why not now? Why not confess the truth? She would be mortified, hurt, and then she'd leave him alone. It would mean the rest of the time she spent in Sydney they'd just carefully avoid one another until she finally went back overseas to work with PMA.

'OK.' The word was spoken very quietly, and Eden's eyes widened. She didn't say anything, instead waiting for him to gather his thoughts, to tell her what it was that had been keeping them apart ever since she'd returned to town.

'When I was an intern—' He broke off, looking into her eyes, seeing the reassurance there, feeling it in her touch. This was it. He was going to do this. He took another breath and slowly let it out. 'When I was an intern, there was an accident—a radiation leak.' His voice was strong, matter-of-fact, as though removing all the emotion from what he was saying helped him to deal with it.

'David!' Eden was astounded, and couldn't help voicing her concerns. 'Were you sick? Poisoned? How bad was it?'

'I suffered radiation sickness, but after a few months I made a complete recovery.'

'Does Sash know?'

'No. I was living in Melbourne and I didn't want to worry her. She'd just started her first job as a teacher and was having the time of her life. She didn't need to be worried about me.'

'So you recovered, then?' Even as she said the words Eden started piecing together all the information she'd inadvertently gathered during the past few days. Such as the number of times David had raised the fact that she would want children. Such as Jacquie saying she'd had trouble conceiving for *years*. Such as David saying there were other reasons for his marriage failure.

'None of us who were affected suffered permanent damage—or so we thought.' David paused, looking down at their entwined fingers. This was it, and he wanted to savour this last moment—her hands against his, the love he saw in her eyes, the way she cared too much. He was going to hurt her and he was sorry for that.

'When Jacquie and I wanted to start a family, we had difficulties conceiving.' He swallowed, forcing himself to go on.

'The radiation had made you sterile.' Eden spoke before he could get the words out.

'Yes.'

She waited, wondering if there was more. When he didn't say anything else, she pressed. 'And?'

'And that's it. I can't father a child, Eden.' He was a little exasperated, and annoyed with her for playing dumb. 'Ever.' He withdrew his hand from hers and clenched his jaw, trying to summon the strength to say the next words. 'So you see, there's no future for us. There never can be. It's over.'

CHAPTER TEN

EDEN frowned, watching him closely. 'What's over?'

'Haven't you heard a single word I've just said?' His exasperation with her increased. 'I can't be with you, Eden. I can't give you the happily-ever-after fairytale you've wanted all your life. I can't father a child. The sterilisation is permanent.'

'So?'

'So! How can you just sit there and say "So"?'

'Simple. Listen and I'll say it again. *So?*'

David was dumbfounded by her reaction. This hadn't been what he'd expected at all. 'Don't you want to have children? Children of your own?'

'Of course I do.'

'Then you're better off without me.'

Eden sat back in her chair for a moment, her drink, the hotel lobby, other guests—everything forgotten as she focused on the man opposite her. 'Are you honestly sitting there and telling me that even though I don't care that you can't father a child we should *still* not be together?'

Her eyes were starting to flash the way they did when she became really mad. David swallowed. He was so attracted to the way she looked, but at the same time wary of her simmering temper. 'Now, Eden. You have to see sense. You're obviously in shock.'

'Don't tell me what I am. I know my own mind, David.'

'Then you'll know that while everything might be fine at the moment, and you might think you can accept this revelation of mine, say it doesn't matter to you, at some point in the future it *won't* be all right. I've been down this road before. I've heard my ex-wife cry herself to sleep because she couldn't have a child. I've signed divorce papers and I've vowed that as far as I was concerned I would never have a family. There is no treatment for this. It's absolute.'

He shifted in his chair, leaning forward, determined to get through to her. 'I know how deeply you feel, Eden. I know how badly things affect you. And even though you say now that you don't mind not having children of your own, one day you will, and one day you will look at me with hatred in your eyes.' *And then you'll leave me.* He didn't say the last words out loud. He couldn't bear to.

It was better all round if they ended things here. Tonight. They'd be able to move on, to find what came next in their lives—because being together would never be an option.

'You're scared.' Eden nodded, as though she'd finally hit the nail on the head. The final piece of the puzzle.

'I'm trying to be rational here, Eden.'

'You are so scared that if you even *try* something new, if you take a chance, you'll end up being hurt again. I can understand that. Honestly I can. I took a chance when I was seventeen and dated you. I loved being with you, spending time together. The hectic times, the fun times, the quiet times. In the beginning I was desperate for you to see me as something more than just a friend. After you'd accepted that things were great. And then…you left. But when you left, what you didn't know was that I was in love with you. Real honest-to-goodness love.'

That stopped his thoughts in their tracks, but

he quickly dismissed her words. 'You were seventeen, Eden. Too young to know what love really is.'

'Perhaps. But I know the pain I felt. I know it took me a very long time to get over you—long after I'd left Sydney. Helping other people, being there for others, was a way I could hide myself, could lock my heart away whilst still doing some good in the world. If I helped other people, then I didn't have to look inwards at myself, didn't have to face the fear that I might be all alone for the rest of my life because the only man I'd ever loved didn't love me back. There was no way I could ever settle for second best. That's just not me.

'I told you that I cried myself to sleep the night I heard of your marriage. I wasn't teasing. You were gone. You'd been taken from me—by some other older, more sophisticated woman. I'd lost you—lost what was never really mine in the first place. I'd lost you. It was then I fully realised my feelings for you were far more than that of a teenage crush or puppy love. They were serious—because to be lusting after another woman's husband was definitely wrong. Yet I couldn't stop myself. You were in me, a part of me, and I'd just locked it all away. If I ignored it, then the pain wasn't as bad.

'I wanted more than anything to get home for Sasha's wedding, because I knew you were divorced. You were free again. I thought that perhaps now…now that I was older, you would finally see me as the woman I'd become. I hoped that you would flirt with me, that you'd take me out into the moonlight, dance with me, kiss me.'

David nodded. 'It wasn't to be.'

'No.' Eden sighed. 'And then Sasha had her accident. My poor, darling Sasha, whom I love like a sister. I came home, unsure of how it would be to see you for the very first time in twelve years, and I have to say it's been the roller-coaster I'd always imagined it would be.' She smiled at him then, and David wasn't sure whether he should relax or stay on alert. 'You are the only man who can make me go weak at the knees with one simple look. You make me smoulder when you touch me. You fill me with fire when you hold me close, when you kiss me, when you look at me with love in your eyes.'

She leaned forward, placing her hands on the table in front of her. 'Only you, David. Only you have ever affected me like this, and only you will continue to affect me like this.' She shook her head. 'If we can't be together then you're sentencing us both to a life alone, a life of living with regrets, when it doesn't need to be that way at all. I don't *care* if you can't have children, and I don't know how to make you believe that.' Her words were spoken in earnest.

'You say that now, but it won't last, Eden. One day you *will* care, and if I can prevent you from experiencing that pain then I will.'

Eden snorted with derision, her eyes flashing fire. 'Oh, how magnanimous of you. Protecting me? How sweet!'

David glanced around them, aware of other patrons. 'You might want to lower your voice.'

'Might I? I might want you to believe me when I say it doesn't matter, but that isn't going to happen either.'

'But you *want* children.' His words were ground out from between his teeth, and she realised that he too was trying to control his temper.

'Yes. Don't you?'

'It doesn't matter what I want. I can't—'

'Be honest, David. It's obvious you *do* want a family of your own, so at least admit it. If not to me, then at least to yourself.'

He shook his head and looked away, wishing they'd risked going up to her room to have this discussion. But he'd thought himself more able to control his undeniable attraction to her in a public place. Besides, he hadn't expected her to react in this manner at all. Then again, this was Eden, and he should have known to expect the unexpected.

'Why do you think I became a paediatrician?'

'Probably the same reasons I did. You love children and you want to help them, to protect them, to guide them. That said, it doesn't change the fact that you're too scared to take the step before you. You're not willing to enter into a relationship with me because one day I might hurt you. You're not willing to believe that the two of us can be happy together—the *two* of us, David. Let's just focus on that for now. I love you, and I know you love me.' Her words had become more insistent and a little louder. 'So *why* can't we move forward? *Why* can't we take that to the next level?'

'You're starting to disturb the other guests.'

'I'm hardly yelling, David, and besides, when you're in love with someone it should make you feel so free, so uninhibited, that you can shout from the rooftops—not knowing who hears, not caring who knows.'

His eyes widened for a moment, and he wondered if she was about to stand up and declare to all and sundry just how she felt about him.

Eden stood, and he held his breath. She walked around to stand beside him before leaning down to kiss him. It was a kiss of desire, of hope and of promise. Then she turned, picked up her coat and bag, and walked calmly to the lifts. He watched as she disappeared from view, the lift taking her away from him.

He wasn't sure how long he sat there, ignoring the people around him as he pondered her words. Did she *really* not care about his secret? Could he believe that she accepted him as he was? That she truly loved him? That she wouldn't leave him in years to come? Could he take a chance on love? True love? Was Eden worth it?

'Yes.'

Two days later, David walked into his sister's hospital room and glanced around. 'Where is she?'

Sasha put down the book she was reading. 'Who?'

'Eden. Who else?'

'I haven't seen her.'

'Sasha,' he warned.

'What? She came to my physio session earlier this morning, but I haven't seen her since. Why? Is there something wrong with a patient?'

'You know darn well what's going on.'

'Ah. Personal, not business. Yes, I do. Eden is more than my best friend, David. She's like a sister to me.'

'Well, if you want to have any hope of making her your real sister, then you'll tell me where she is.' He stalked around the room, agitated and tired. 'I've been trying to call her for the past two days. First of all the hotel took my messages, saying she didn't want to be disturbed. And now I've just called and they've informed me that Dr Caplan isn't staying there any more.'

Sasha nodded. 'Have you tried her cellphone?'

'It just goes through to voicemail. Where *is* she?' He felt so dejected, and slumped into a chair. 'I've stuffed up, Sash. She won't talk to me. She's avoiding me.'

'Haven't you seen her on the ward? I thought she was a visiting medical officer.'

'She is, but whilst she's been in to see the patients she does it when she *knows* I won't be on the ward. She knows my schedule inside out— when I have clinic, when I have meetings—and she uses it to her advantage. This morning Dart was jumping around, all happy and cheery because Dr Eden had just done a magic trick and pulled some money from his ear. Then I go to see Chelsea and she tells me that she and Eden shared a hot chocolate this morning as they talked about Paris.'

'Isn't she the young girl who wasn't eating?'

'Yes.' David raked a hand through his hair and stood to start pacing again. 'Yesterday I spent a lot of time trying to track her down, narrowly missing her. "She was just here." "Oh, David, you just missed her." Everyone likes her. Everyone thinks the world of her—'

'It's you that she loves,' Sasha pointed out.

'She has a funny way of showing it.'

'How do you feel about *her*, David? Eden's sure you love her, but that you're too scared to do anything about it.'

'I am. I was.'

'In love with her or scared?'

'I *am* in love with her and I *was* scared.' He'd been such a fool—a fool in love. And love could be blind, couldn't it? He just hadn't known what he was doing, fumbling around like a...well, like a fool.

'So what are you going to do about it?'

'A lot. But first I need to find her.' He came and gently sat on the bed next to his sister. 'Help me, Sash.'

'I'll call her.' Sasha picked up the phone by her bed and dialled an outside line before entering Eden's number. 'Hi, there,' she said a moment later. 'Where are you?' A pause. David looked hopefully at his sister. 'Uh-huh.' Sasha's gaze met his. 'Oh? Really?' Another pause. 'Eden, I'm sorry. No. No. I quite understand. Yes, yes, he is here with me. Do you want to—'

David eagerly held his hand out for the receiver, but Sasha didn't relinquish it.

'No?' she continued. 'All right, then. Yes. OK. Call me if you want to talk.' Sasha hung up the phone and glared at her brother. 'You had better fix that.'

'What? What just happened?'

'She doesn't want to talk to you.'

'What? Why not?' Panic gripped him and he found it difficult to swallow. 'Where is she, Sasha?'

'I promised her I wouldn't tell you.'

'What? This isn't primary school. We aren't playing kid games. This is my *life*.'

'Eden's too.'

David began to pace around the room. What was Eden doing? Playing hard to get?

'She just needs to sort herself out, that's all.'

'And what if she leaves? What if she runs away again?'

'What if she does?' Sasha countered. 'What would you do, David?'

'Go after her.' He didn't even need to think of his answer. He needed Eden, was desperate for Eden, and now that he'd realised that he wanted to go to her, apologise and beg her to take him back. 'Come on, Sash. Tell me where she is. We need to talk. We need to sort this out. She doesn't understand how much I need her in my life. I have to tell her.'

'Well, you're going to have to wait a few more days, at least. Unless…' Sasha smiled widely at her brother, wanting the two people she'd loved for most of her life to get their act together.

'Unless?'

'Unless you're smart and you figure out where she might have gone. Let's see if I can't help you narrow down the parameters. Who does Eden know in Sydney? You. Me. Well, she isn't staying with either of us. Hmm… Who else does she know here? Who else would she go and visit with to reconcile the past?'

David hit his forehead and shook his head, before kissing his sister's cheek.

'You'd better tell her you love her, David,' Sasha called as he bolted for the door.

'I'll shout it from the rooftops,' he returned with a bright grin.

David knocked on his tennis partner's front door with complete impatience. He hadn't bothered waiting for someone to open the large front gates, instead had quickly scaled the front brick wall. Hal answered, surprised to see a dishevelled David standing there.

'Is Eden here?' he asked eagerly.

'I'm sorry. You've just missed her. She's gone shopping with her mother.'

He couldn't believe he'd just missed her! *Again!*

'Come in, son.' Hal invited him, and they went into the living room. 'You've obviously heard that Eden's staying with us?'

'I've not long realised that.'

'She came round late last night and asked if she could come home.' Hal shook his head, tears welling in his eyes. 'It's as though everything really is in the past—that it has all been forgiven and forgotten. I feel as though I have my family back.' He clapped David on the back. 'And we owe it all to you.'

'To me?'

'Yes. You brought her over, got her to talk to us.'

'I didn't do anything, Hal. It was all Eden. I merely provided moral support.'

Hal nudged him and winked. 'Looked like more than moral support to me. So, what's the deal? You in love with my Eden?'

'As a matter of fact, yes.' David's answer momentarily stunned Hal.

'Really? I was only trying to tease you.' Hal gulped and quickly processed the information. 'Well, that's beaut, then.' He offered his hand to David and pumped it proudly. 'If you can tame my daughter, get her to settle down, we'd be forever grateful.'

David's smile was one of slight relief. He'd found out where Eden was staying. She was all right. She hadn't left town. She hadn't given up on him. 'I doubt *anyone* can tame Eden. Besides, I think she's perfect just the way she is.'

Hal beamed. 'Welcome to the family, son.'

David needed to prove to Eden that he was worth taking a risk with. Sasha wanted them to be together, and so did Hal, but it was Eden who mattered and David had to keep reminding himself that he hadn't won *her* over...yet. He needed to convince her that he was serious, that he believed in her, believed in them, and that despite what the future might hold he wanted it to be the two of them together—for ever.

But how? How could he? After a moment David stood. 'Listen, Hal, do you have a ladder I could borrow?'

'I'm so glad the hospital let you come,' Eden said to Sasha as she gathered the dinner plates.

'You and me both. Sister thought as I'd managed to survive the other night at a restaurant, I could manage a sedate family dinner.'

'It's like old times,' Gretchen said, helping her daughter. 'Only David's missing. Where did David say he was tonight, Hal?'

Hal thought for a moment, then shrugged. 'He said he had some business to take care of.'

'It was a wonderful meal, Mrs Caplan,' Sasha commented, wanting to change the subject. Her brother had called her to let her know what he had planned, which was why Sasha had insisted on wangling an invitation to dinner. She wasn't going to miss this moment for anything.

'Thank you, dear. Todd, take those plates from Eden—you too, Hal. The two of you can be on dish duty tonight.'

'Well, if it's the men's turn,' Robert said, 'I'd better help, too.'

'They only have to stack the dishwasher,' Eden said. 'How hard is that?'

'For your father and brother?' Gretchen said. 'It could take quite a while. They both have their own system, and they argue over which one is the most effective. Now, why don't you get the things you bought today, Eden, while I wheel Sasha into the living room? Then we can have a bit of a girly time looking at clothes and shoes.'

'Mum bought me way too much. I don't know what I'm going to do with it all.' Eden started towards the stairs, but stopped when she heard a strange noise. 'What on earth is that?' she asked, heading over to the window. Gretchen followed, and both of them peered out.

Dogs up and down the street were beginning to bark, but the noise continued and it sounded very close. Eden went to the front door and walked outside, down the steps onto the grass, searching for the sound. She turned and glanced up at the roof, her heart catching in her throat.

'David! What are you doing up there?'

'Serenading you,' he called back, and began to sing once more. He was standing on the roof of her father's house, balancing very carefully. He was wearing a tuxedo and held one single long stemmed rose in his hands.

The rest of her family came out, with Todd and Robert carrying Sasha's wheelchair down the steps.

'You're supposed to be on the ground and I'm supposed to be up high if you're going to serenade correctly,' she called, but he continued to sing. Badly.

It *was* awful, and he was fumbling a lot of the words, which only made him sound worse, but she loved every wrong note he sang. Eden laughed at the total ridiculousness of the man, clapping her hands in delight, unable to believe he was doing what he was doing. When David broke out of his shell he *broke out*!

'At least we have a doctor around if he falls,' Hal commented.

'Come down!' she called, but he continued singing—if you could call it that. 'You're scaring the animals in the neighbourhood,' she tried, and finally he finished.

Then he looked down at her and smiled.

'I love you, Eden,' he said, and then lifted his head and yelled to the entire neighbourhood, 'I love Eden Caplan.'

She laughed, unable to believe he was *actually* shouting from the rooftops that he loved her.

'Why is he up there?' Gretchen asked. 'What's wrong with the ground?'

'It's romantic.' Sasha sighed, and clasped her hands to her chest.

'Oh,' was all Gretchen said.

Eden saw the ladder, and knew if he wasn't going to come down then she was going to go up—and that was exactly what she did, climbing carefully onto the roof. She stood and headed over to him, watching where she was putting her feet.

'Be careful,' he said when he spotted her, and reached out a hand, grasping hers and steadying her when she missed her step. When they were next to each other, he looked down into her eyes. 'I've missed you,' he whispered.

'I've missed you, too,' she said. 'It's just like you to be so literal.'

'Hey, you wanted me to shout it from the

rooftops and I have. The serenading was something I came up with all by myself.' The smile on his face began to fade. 'You've said a few times that Sasha is the only person who's ever really cared about you, and I want you to know that's not entirely true. She's not the *only* person, Eden. I've cared about you for far longer than I've been willing to admit to myself. I'm sorry, Eden. Sorry for hurting you, for rejecting you, for not listening to you. Can you please forgive me?'

'Why?'

'Because I love you. *I love her!*' he shouted again, and she laughed.

'You're crazy.'

'You've taught me everything I know in that department.' He waited a beat, then said seriously, 'I'm sorry about the other day. I was just so overwhelmed that you weren't put off by my revelation that I didn't want to believe what I was hearing.'

'I love you, David. *You.* If we can't have our own children, that's fine.' She shrugged one elegant shoulder. 'We'll adopt.'

He widened his eyes. 'Just like that? Adopt?'

Eden's smile continued to grow as she pushed

her fingers lovingly through his hair. 'Have you forgotten where I've been working? Many of my assignments have been at orphanages. There are so many children out there with no one to love them. You and I both know that love is what matters, not bloodlines.'

He nodded. 'Every child needs love.'

'And we'll give it. Look at your friends Chloe and Michael. They've adopted a little Tarparniian boy, and he probably won't be their last.' She laced her hands behind his head. 'We can *do* this, David. We really can. I believe it with all my heart. We *can* be parents—parents who will shower their children with love.'

David couldn't believe how incredible this woman was. She gave and she gave and she just kept on giving. He vowed right then and there to always give back to her. He would support her, help her to remain strong and support the gift she had. Together they could do so much, share so much of themselves, so much of their love.

'Eden, I need you in my life. I've loved you for so long, but I was just too preoccupied with my own sadness to notice. I let it eat away at my life, and because of that I almost missed my chance at true happiness.'

She smiled at him. 'You didn't miss it, sexy boy. I'm still here.'

'Marry me? Be my wild-child wife?'

'Wife, eh?'

'I want you to marry me. No.' He stopped, and her heart caught in her throat. 'I *need* you to be my wife.'

She looked into his eyes, seeing the commitment, and the love, as well as the passion and the desire. 'Really?' she whispered.

'Yes.' He laughed. '*Please*, yes.'

'Why?'

'Because you're the other half of me,' he replied. 'Where we live, how many children we adopt, where we work—that's all semantics. I realise that now. I need to know you'll be with me, Eden. Side by side. Together. For ever.'

'I love you,' she said. 'So very, very much, David.'

'Is that a yes?'

'You bet it is. Besides, after your public display of affection, how could I refuse?'

At that, his mouth met hers.

This was the very beginning of their life as Mr and Mrs Perfectly Happy—which was what Eden had been striving for her whole life.

'Are you two ever coming down?' Sasha called with excited impatience, making Eden laugh.

Eden didn't rush to end the kiss, but when he lifted his mouth from hers she allowed David to help her towards the ladder. He kissed her lips once more.

'After you, my wild-child.'

'Thank you, my tone-deaf serenader.'

When they were on the ground, and after they'd been congratulated and hugged by their family, David took her in his arms once more.

'We are so perfect for each other.'

'Mmm,' Eden said, pressing her mouth to his. 'Told you so.'

MEDICAL™

Large Print

Titles for the next six months…

May

COUNTRY MIDWIFE, CHRISTMAS BRIDE	Abigail Gordon
GREEK DOCTOR: ONE MAGICAL CHRISTMAS	Meredith Webber
HER BABY OUT OF THE BLUE	Alison Roberts
A DOCTOR, A NURSE: A CHRISTMAS BABY	Amy Andrews
SPANISH DOCTOR, PREGNANT MIDWIFE	Anne Fraser
EXPECTING A CHRISTMAS MIRACLE	Laura Iding

June

SNOWBOUND: MIRACLE MARRIAGE	Sarah Morgan
CHRISTMAS EVE: DOORSTEP DELIVERY	Sarah Morgan
HOT-SHOT DOC, CHRISTMAS BRIDE	Joanna Neil
CHRISTMAS AT RIVERCUT MANOR	Gill Sanderson
FALLING FOR THE PLAYBOY MILLIONAIRE	Kate Hardy
THE SURGEON'S NEW-YEAR WEDDING WISH	Laura Iding

July

POSH DOC, SOCIETY WEDDING	Joanna Neil
THE DOCTOR'S REBEL KNIGHT	Melanie Milburne
A MOTHER FOR THE ITALIAN'S TWINS	Margaret McDonagh
THEIR BABY SURPRISE	Jennifer Taylor
NEW BOSS, NEW-YEAR BRIDE	Lucy Clark
GREEK DOCTOR CLAIMS HIS BRIDE	Margaret Barker

MILLS & BOON®

MEDICAL™

Large Print

August

September

October

MILLS & BOON®

millsandboon.co.uk Community

Join Us!

The Community is the perfect place to meet and chat to kindred spirits who love books and reading as much as you do, but it's also the place to:

- Get the inside scoop from authors about their latest books
- Learn how to write a romance book with advice from our editors
- Help us to continue publishing the best in women's fiction
- Share your thoughts on the books we publish
- Befriend other users

Forums: Interact with each other as well as authors, editors and a whole host of other users worldwide.

Blogs: Every registered community member has their own blog to tell the world what they're up to and what's on their mind.

Book Challenge: We're aiming to read 5,000 books and have joined forces with The Reading Agency in our inaugural Book Challenge.

Profile Page: Showcase yourself and keep a record of your recent community activity.

Social Networking: We've added buttons at the end of every post to share via digg, Facebook, Google, Yahoo, technorati and de.licio.us.

www.millsandboon.co.uk

APL		CCS	
Cen		Ear	
Mob		Cou	
ALL		Jub	
WH		CHE	
Aid		Bel	
Fin		Fol	
Can	13·3·12	STO	
Til		HCL	